PROMISES

Other books by Carolyn Brown:

Love Is
A Falling Star
All the Way from Texas
The Yard Rose
The Ivy Tree
Lily's White Lace
That Way Again
The Wager
Trouble in Paradise
The PMS Club

The *Love's Valley Historical Romance* Series:

Redemption
Choices
Absolution
Chances

The *Promised Land Romance* Series:

Willow
Velvet
Gypsy
Garnet
Augusta

The *Land Rush Romance* Series:

Emma's Folly
Violet's Wish
Maggie's Mistake
Just Grace

PROMISES

•

Carolyn Brown

AVALON BOOKS
NEW YORK

Published by Thomas Bouregy & Co., Inc.
160 Madison Avenue, New York, NY 10016

Library of Congress Cataloging-in-Publication Data

Brown, Carolyn, 1948–
Promises / Carolyn Brown.
p. cm.
ISBN 0-8034-9806-3 (acid-free paper)
1. United States—History—Civil War, 1861–1865—Fiction.
2. Pennsylvania—Fiction. I. Title.

PS3552.R685275P76 2006
813'.54—dc22

2006018524

PRINTED IN THE UNITED STATES OF AMERICA
ON ACID-FREE PAPER
BY HADDON CRAFTSMEN, BLOOMSBURG, PENNSYLVANIA

To Charles
Always and forever

Chapter One

Indigo Hamilton stepped out of the enclosed buggy and picked up her bridal nosegay of pale peach roses picked fresh that morning and arranged with streaming satin ribbons. The article about the wedding had been written already and taken to the *Shirleysburg Herald*, and would run in next week's issue. Everything at the Hamilton farm in Love's Valley was ready for the reception following the most lavish wedding since before the war. Absolutely nothing had been left to chance.

"You are beautiful, little sister." Monroe Hamilton offered his arm to the bride. "Is this the same lady who feared she'd never get a husband because she was taller than most of the young men in Huntingdon County, Pennsylvania?"

"The one and same. At least I got one in Huntingdon County and didn't have to marry a Rebel like all you men in the family."

"Careful now. A bride is supposed to be sweet and kind

on her wedding day, and you don't want all of your brothers up in arms because you said mean things about their wives. Me included," Monroe said. Indigo had always been too outspoken and spoiled for her own good. She'd hated all things Southern, so it really stuck in her craw when all her brothers brought home Rebel wives after the war. The fact that their cousin, Ellie, who'd lived with them since the great Chambersburg fire, also married a Southerner didn't help matters.

"I will be sweet as honey to my *Yankee* husband," Indigo declared. "I'll tolerate the Southern wives for Momma's sake, but I don't want to spoil my wedding day by talking about them. I'm so glad to be moving away from Love's Valley. I bet Thomas is already waiting at the front of the altar."

"And I bet his eyes are going to pop right out when he sees you." Monroe patted her hand. He'd hoped she'd find a husband who could tame her. He had serious doubts that Thomas had enough fire in him to do the job.

"They should," Indigo said. "This dress was featured in *Harper's Bazaar* just last spring. Do you have any idea how much Chantilly lace is on the gigot sleeves alone, not to mention this ruffle? Imported lace does not come cheap, brother, so when you pay the bill out of my account, be prepared to suck air for an hour," she teased.

"Don't tell me right now. All those fancy terms you just used are enough to boggle my poor little brain for one day. Just let me live in ignorance. If you told me the price of all that foo-foo, I'm sure I'd drop dead in my tracks. It's probably more than that new horse I bought last week."

"It's more than five of those horses." She knocked on the church doors, and her other two older brothers, Rueben and

Reed, serving as ushers, threw the doors open. Organ music filled the entire church, and everyone stood on their feet.

Indigo loved every minute of the attention. What she liked best was the look on Thomas Brewster's face as he watched her stroll up the center aisle. Her groom looked as if he'd been pole-axed to see such a frothy creation coming closer and closer. It did her heart good to see that she'd truly rendered him senseless. She just hoped he wasn't speechless when their priest asked him to repeat his vows.

"Who gives this woman to be married to this man?" Father Paul asked.

"Her family and I do." Monroe took her hand from his arm and put it in Thomas' outstretched hand. "Treat her well, Thomas Brewster," he said very quietly.

"I will," Thomas said seriously.

"Dearly beloved, we are gathered here this glorious morning," the priest began.

Yes, morning, Indigo thought a bit crossly. *I'd much rather have had a late evening wedding with a romantic candlelight reception, but the church doesn't think that's proper. Weddings should be held in the mornings. I wonder why?*

"Let us pray." The priest bowed his head and began to read a long, long wedding passage from his book.

While the priest delivered the first prayer, Flannon Sullivan slipped in and sat in the back pew. He'd been the buggy driver, bringing Indigo and Monroe to the wedding. The rest of the Hamiltons and Sullivans were at the front of the church. It had been decided at rehearsal that he would sit at the back since he'd been chosen to drive the newly wedded couple to the reception.

His sister, Douglass Sullivan, had married into the family the year before. She and their brother, Colum, who'd also lost his mind and married into the Yankee family, had talked him into staying in Love's Valley through the winter months to help build homes and train horses.

Flannon dropped his head and shut his eyes for the prayer, but his thoughts wandered. Tommy Brewster must be a sucker for pain if he was going to stand there before Father Paul, all the people of Shirleysburg, the family, and even God and vow to live with that shrew of a woman until death parted them. Flannon could easily see that Indigo's beauty had turned Thomas' head: a full bosom and well-rounded hips, all that dark hair with copper highlights, eyes as dark as sapphires, and a waist so small Flannon could have spanned it with his two hands. Not that he ever would. Sweet Jesus, he couldn't be within five feet of her for more than five minutes without a war erupting.

At least Thomas would have something nice to look upon when she was ranting and raving and being the spoiled brat she was most of the time. And the best part was that she'd be living in Shirleysburg when they returned from their wedding trip to Philadelphia for a week. If she'd been planning to live at the farm in Love's Valley, Flannon would be joining his older brother, Patrick, and his mother when they left for northeast Texas the next morning. There wasn't enough dirt in all of Texas or money in the world to make him winter in a household where he'd have to be in close contact with Miss Indigo Hamilton. By the time spring rolled around someone would be dead.

There'd been no love lost between them the previous year when he and Colum had tracked down Douglass in Love's Valley, Pennsylvania. Their first confrontation had been in the middle of a fist fight. Flannon had been busy trying to peel Cousin Ellie off Colum's back when Indigo all but broke his nose with her fist. She'd been surly then, and if anything, her tongue had been honed even more in the past months. Yes sir, Tommy Brewster was deaf, dumb, or just plumb crazy. Maybe all three.

Flannon raised his head to look over those bowed in prayer so he could see the rest of the family seated in the front pew. Laura Hamilton, mother to Monroe, Rueben, and Reed as well as Indigo. How someone as sweet-natured and kind as that woman had given birth to Indigo was an enigma. It was like a bunny rabbit spawning a rabid coyote. Next to Laura sat Flannon's sister, Douglass, and her husband, Monroe. Flannon's mother, Mary Margaret, held Douglass and Monroe's new baby, Ford. The oldest Sullivan son, Patrick, sat beside her.

On the next pew Flannon's brother, Colum, sat with his wife, Ellie, cousin to the Hamiltons. Ellie had come to live with Laura when the Yankees burned her home in the great Chambersburg fire. It was a pure miracle she and Colum had ever gotten together. If it hadn't been for the fact that she'd been kidnapped and Colum had been sent to rescue her or else endure Douglass' wrath for all eternity, it would never have happened.

Beside them were Rueben and Adelida, and Reed and Geneva, and their daughter, Angelina. Quite a big family, but not as large as the Sullivans in north Texas. Six sons and then Douglass tagging along at the end of the line. Now two of the seven lived in Love's Valley.

Thank goodness I'm not one of those who've forsaken their roots for love. And I never will!

* * *

Indigo fidgeted through the prayer. Her feet began to ache. Thank goodness she'd opted for a simple pair of white velvet slippers instead of high-heeled wedding boots. She was five feet, six inches tall, and if she'd worn boots she would have towered over Tommy, who was the same height. She'd even dressed her hair with a center part and bun at the nape of her neck, and set the waxed orange blossom headpiece holding her tulle veil at the back of her head to keep from being taller than Thomas. A perfect bride, wedding, and reception shouldn't have women whispering behind their fans that she was a giant and the groom a dwarf.

"Amen," Father Paul finally intoned.

Indigo hadn't listened to the words. Instead she'd envisioned the three-tiered wedding cake with orange blossoms and roses on the top. Everyone in Shirleysburg, Pennsylvania, would talk for years about this wedding. Not one of her brothers, even with their exciting tales of how they'd come to be married to Southern women, could top what would be said about her extravagant wedding. Maybe it would bring some of the former prewar grandeur back to the area.

"Now if anyone is in disagreement with this wedding, anyone who has cause to believe that the wedding should not continue, let him now speak or forever hold his peace," Father Paul said and waited.

Reed had teased her that he was going to stand right up in the second pew and announce that the wedding should not take place because Tommy Brewster was besotted and not in his right mind. Indigo bit the inside of her lip thinking about the good-natured ribbing she'd gotten from her three brothers. Not one of them would dare even clear their throats behind her or they'd suffer her wrath for all eternity. She was in her glory, and no one would or could spoil it.

Besides, there were no objections to the wedding. Why would there be? She and Tommy had known each other since they were babies. The four years he'd fought against the awful Rebels was the only time they hadn't lived right under each other's noses. So why did Father Paul hesitate so long?

Father Paul had actually lost his place in the wedding book. He'd flipped two pages at once. When he looked down to continue the ceremony, he was on the wrong page. He flipped forward and then realized what had hap pened, so he slowly turned two pages back and found the next portion right there in the middle.

"Then." He cleared his throat.

Before he could say another word, the double doors at the back of the church flew open. From the silhouette framed against the bright sunlight, Father Paul could see the intruder was a woman in billowing skirts, a latecomer who didn't have the grace to sneak in through one door and sit in the back pew.

"Then we shall go on since there are no objections," he said, hoping the woman would shut the doors and find a seat.

"I have an objection," the shadowy image said in a soft Southern voice that carried all the way up the aisle.

Flannon jerked his head around to see who had the nerve to say something like that at Indigo's wedding. Lord, she'd better have a hatchet hiding in the folds of her skirt or underneath that little boy baby's blanket. She'd need that and more to fend off Indigo's temper.

Father Paul blushed. He'd overheard the Hamilton brothers teasing their sister, but this didn't seem like a joke. Matter of fact, it felt real.

"And your objection, young lady?" Father Paul asked in a booming voice.

Every eye in the church left the handsome groom and gorgeous bride in the front of the church and looked toward the lady carrying a baby boy up the aisle on her hip. Indigo let go of Tommy's hand, spun around as far as her corset and stays would allow her, and glared at the woman. If one of her brothers were responsible for this act, they were all dead men.

"Maudie?" Thomas whispered.

Indigo looked at Thomas. His face had gone ashy gray. He knew the woman. Just what had he done to spoil her wedding? Anger filled her heart. Her first impulse was to march down the aisle and yank the woman bald.

"Thomas Brewster?" The woman raised an eyebrow in question.

"Maudie, is that you?" Thomas left Indigo's side and rushed down the aisle.

"Tommy, they told me you were dead. They said you were killed at that last battle. But I knew you were alive. I could feel it in my bones. I would have known if you were dead. My heart would have died with you."

"But Maudie, when I came back to the plantation, it was gone. Burned to the ground, and the townspeople told me the whole family perished." He was afraid to touch her for fear she'd disappear. He'd put the first love of his life out of his mind as much as possible when he'd returned home, and here she stood at the worst possible moment.

"Looks like we both were misled," Maudie said. "Now

what are we going to do about this, Tommy, darlin'? Father, this man is already married. And this is his son. We were married two and a half years ago, in the Catholic church in Virginia just before the end of the war."

The bones in Indigo's legs disappeared, and it took every bit of willpower she possessed to keep from falling into a heap of white lace and satin. If she'd had to speak or die, she'd have had to ask Father Paul to administer last rites. She dropped her bouquet on the floor. Darn Thomas Brewster to hell for all eternity! He'd just made her the laughingstock of the whole area. Not once had he mentioned having a Rebel wife, even if he did think she was dead.

"Is that the truth, Thomas?" Father Paul asked in a hushed tone.

"Yes, sir, it is," Thomas reached out to touch Maudie's face and take his son into his arms, an absolute miniature of his father. He'd be about a year and a half old if Thomas' speedy calculations were right.

"Then I suppose we'd better call this wedding off then until this is all straightened out," Father Paul said.

"I'm so sorry." Tommy turned to Indigo. "I thought she was dead and I . . ."

"And you never even told me you'd married a Southern woman?" Indigo whispered hoarsely around a lump of pure old mad lodged in her throat. She wanted to scream or at least kick something, but the only person standing with her was the priest.

"It was in the past and too painful to talk about, and you hate Southerners so I figured you'd throw a fit," Tommy said.

"I think maybe we should all leave the church now,"

Monroe announced. "Perhaps Tommy and his wife, and Indigo, need some time alone to sort this out."

The congregation filed out of the church in stunned silence. All but Mable Cunningham, a gray-haired woman who'd been in Shirleysburg the past eighty-two years. She'd been sitting beside Flannon, and her first words after a loud snort were, "Poor Laura. That girl is going to be a handful."

Flannon waited in the back pew, not knowing what to do. There'd be no caravan to Love's Valley for the reception now. He stared at Maudie. She was a beauty. Red hair, pale complexion: a tiny, wispy woman with the softest voice Flannon had ever heard. If she'd been living on the next ranch in Texas, he would have sure made an effort to get across the property lines to visit her. As bad as he hated Indigo, though, a pang of sorrow pierced his heart for her. No woman, not even one with a wicked tongue, deserved that kind of shock. She was as pale as a corpse standing up there, so rigid she looked like she had a steel rod running from her toes to the top of her head. In bewilderment she watched everyone leave the church.

"You bring her home when it's over," his mother whispered as she passed.

Flannon nodded in agreement, because he'd never refuse his mother anything. But he sure didn't want to be the one on the receiving end of Indigo's temper when the truth settled and she found herself literally jilted at the altar.

Good grief, she'll be coming back to the farm.

Suddenly he wished he hadn't promised his brother and sister he'd stay in Love's Valley for the winter. Sure, he had pity for the woman. Who wouldn't? But everything in him wished he could take back his promise.

"Maudie, oh, Maudie, I can't believe you are alive." Tommy kept touching her arm.

"You gave me your word!" Indigo yelled. "How could you ruin my day? You are a scoundrel, Tommy. A liar. You promised to love me forever."

"But I gave it thinking my wife was dead," Tommy said. "How did you figure out . . . ," he started, and Maudie reached up to kiss him briefly on the lips.

That should have been Indigo's wedding kiss. Maudie looked as if she could have Tommy for breakfast, dinner, and supper and still be hungry for more. Tommy could scarcely take his eyes from the redhead or the little boy who was most certainly a Brewster.

"Tommy Brewster, don't you stand there on my wedding day and kiss another woman!" Indigo stomped on her rose bouquet and marched down the aisle to face them. "And don't you act like everything is just wonderful because you found your long-lost husband, Maudie Whoever-you-are."

"I'm sorry to ruin your wedding, but I'm not sorry to find my husband," Maudie said to Indigo. "I'd fight any one or anything for him. Let's go, Tommy."

"I wouldn't fight a fly for him now. He's ruined my life. You can have him." Indigo picked up her skirt and started toward the door.

"I just came to see if your brother had survived the war so he could get to know his nephew. I arrived this morning, and the man at the hotel said you were getting married. Do you love this woman? Tommy, I won't stand in your way if you do. We can divorce. The church would understand."

"No!" Indigo turned abruptly. "No, I wouldn't marry a

divorced man. I couldn't, and besides I don't want him. Not now."

"And no, I don't want a divorce. I love you, Maudie. I just thought you were dead. I am sorry, Indigo." He didn't look at his bride but at his wife.

"Get out of here and leave me alone." Indigo's tone was icy.

Tommy ushered Maudie out of the church where Charlie, his brother, waited with a buggy. They'd straighten it all out. A son. Maudie. His heart soared.

"What are you still doing here?" Indigo turned her rising rage on Flannon, who'd stood up in the back pew. Of all the people in the world who had to overhear that conversation, it would have to be the youngest Sullivan brother, the one she despised the most. That was just the icing on the worst day of her life.

"They left me to bring you home," he said bluntly. "I sure didn't ask for the job. It just fell on me since I was the one who was supposed to drive the bride and groom to the reception."

"The reception!" Indigo slammed her bouquet to the floor. "Surely all these people and the Brewsters won't go out there for a reception."

"I doubt it. I imagine the bunch of us will be eating leftovers for a week. Guess we can feed it to the hired hands when they come Monday morning. That should get rid of a lot of it," he said.

"Men!" She snorted. "Just take me to the stage station. I'm leaving Shirleysburg. I'll go to Philadelphia by myself and . . ."

"You're going to get in that rig out there, and I'm taking you to Love's Valley, Indigo Hamilton. Right down the main street of Shirleysburg and over the ridge like we always go after church. You're not running from your problems. I don't like you one bit better than you like me. You're a spoiled rotten brat. We both know how we feel about the other, but today is not your fault. So you're not going to tuck your tail between your legs and run," he said.

"I'd expect a Rebel to talk dirty like that. A Yankee wouldn't mention a woman's legs, much less in the same sentence with the word *tail.* And you of all people calling me spoiled. That's a classic case of the pot calling the kettle black." She glared at him.

"No filth intended. Just pure fact. That's what you'd be doing. And honey, there's not a man or woman in the world who'd win a contest for spoiled if you were in it. If a body could buy you for what you're worth and sell you for what you think you're worth, he'd be a millionaire," he said.

She fought back the tears of anger. Flannon Sullivan sure wouldn't see her cry. "Don't you ever call me honey. Take me home and then you can go to hell." She plucked her veil from her head, tossed it on the ground, and walked on it as she marched resolutely across the churchyard.

Flannon held his hand out at the carriage door. She completely ignored it, swept her ridiculously long train up in the seat beside her, and slammed the door hard enough to rock the whole wagon. He hoisted himself up on the driver's seat, slapped the reins against the horses' flanks, and turned the rig around to go back to Love's Valley. He would have rather been in a fierce battle against the Union soldiers than riding in a rig with Indigo Hamilton. Especially one decorated with flowers, tulle, and a big sign reading "Just Married" on the back.

Chapter Two

Flannon wondered if Indigo was planning a murder. To his way of thinking, Tommy Brewster and that new bride of his had better lie low for a few weeks. After ordering him to take her home and then deciding where he should spend eternity, she'd stewed in silence the whole way. When he stopped in front of the house, she bundled the train to her wedding dress over her arm and stormed up the stairs without a word to any of her family members. In ten minutes she came back down to the parlor where everyone sat in stunned silence, even the two babies, not uttering a whimper. She'd changed into a pair of trousers, a faded flannel shirt, and work boots and had taken her hair down and braided it into a long rope that hung down her back beneath an old straw hat.

"You can feed that wedding cake to the hogs if you want or save it for the hired hands that will arrive Monday morning to work on cluttering up our valley with houses for these Southern women. I don't care what happens to it, but I don't want it left where I can see it. Ellie, will you take care of sending back all those wedding gifts in the foyer? Would someone go to my room and get rid of that wedding dress? Put it in a trunk in the attic. Burn it. I don't care. I just don't want to see it again. After the shortages in the war, I hate to see good food go to waste, so what will keep until Monday let the hired help eat it. Now I'm going to the barn and muck out horse stalls the rest of the day. I won't hear a word about this fiasco and I mean it. Not ever. From anyone. I don't want your pity. Momma says hard work will take care of things. I hope it does." She disappeared out the back door, slamming it so hard the dishes rattled in the kitchen cabinets.

"Whew!" Reed gasped. "And here we were afraid we'd have to console her bawling spells for a month."

"I told you!" Geneva, his wife, slapped at his arm. "A strong woman like Indigo doesn't pout. She gets mad. She kicks. She fights. If she were a man she'd get rip-roaring drunk, but she doesn't pout. She'll be all right, that one will."

"Yes, she will," Mary Margaret said. "Strong women don't whine, do they, Douglass?"

"Unless it benefits them." Douglass smiled.

The room grew quiet. Douglass' smile faded as she held her son, Ford, close to her chest. She'd come to Love's Valley from Texas not even a year before. A worthless Yankee had led her down the daisy path of moral destruction, or would have liked to but she'd taken the only option she had and thwarted his plans. There she was sitting in the middle of the road on her trunk when Monroe Hamilton, another Yankee but at least a re-spectable one, appeared like the answer to a prayer, on his way to Pennsylvania. Which was a long, long way from her brothers who would be itching to put her in a convent for her misjudgment. By the time Monroe had escorted her through thick and thin, they'd fallen in love. Indigo hated her.

Ellie reached over and took Colum's hand, squeezing it gently. She'd despised all things Southern after Rebels burned her home in Chambersburg, Pennsylvania. At least until Colum had changed her mind. He was Douglass' brother and had rescued Ellie when death was breathing hot right in her face. Even then she wasn't going to like the man, but her heart had a different set of rules. It didn't care that Colum was a Rebel, that he was half-Irish or half-Mexican. It just took off on its own, and she fell in love with the man. Indigo hated him.

Rueben slipped his arm around Adelida, his bride from the Louisiana bayou country. He'd been in that part of the world after the war helping with reconstruction. The day he was leaving to go home to Love's Valley, he'd tried to prevent a bank robbery and gotten a terrible thump on the head for his efforts. When he awoke, he had stitches in his forehead, no memory, and a Southern wife. In the course of a trip from there to Love's Valley, he regained his memory, lost the stitches, and found he'd fallen in love with Adelida even if she wasn't truly his legal wife. Indigo absolutely hated her.

The youngest brother, Reed, put his arm around his wife, Geneva. The baby, Angelina, slept peacefully in her mother's arms. A few weeks before, Reed had been on his way home from Savannah, Georgia, in a stagecoach because he could not abide ship travel. The only other passenger was a big, dirty woman and before morning he and the fat lady were tossed out on the side of the road in the middle of a heist. The next morning he found out that Geneva wasn't fat; she was pregnant, and Angelina was only minutes away from birth. By the time they'd traveled together a month, he'd fallen in love. Now Geneva and Angelina were part of the Hamilton family. Indigo hated Geneva.

Mary Margaret Sullivan patted her son, Patrick, on the shoulder. Thank goodness he was in love with a woman in Texas. She didn't know if she could bear giving another of her children to Love's Valley. It had already claimed Douglass and Colum. Douglass loved Monroe. Colum loved Ellie. Someday there would be trains between DeKalb, Texas, and Shirleysburg, Pennsylvania. For now it was a long, exhausting trip from the ranch in northern Texas to the valley in southern Pennsylvania. At least she didn't have to worry about Flannon. He'd be staying the winter to help his sister and brother, but he'd be coming home next spring. After all, Indigo hated him.

"Laura, I know this is a poor time for me to ask you this question, but I've been putting it off long enough." Mary Margaret snapped open a black lace fan and stirred the stale parlor air around her face.

"Yes?" Laura raised an eyebrow. All of her children were supposed to be married and settled by this time today. Had she been choosing a mate for any one of her sons, she would not have chosen a single one of her daughters-in-law. Not Douglass for sure. Not Adelida on a bet. Certainly not Geneva. But she would have chosen wrong because those women were exactly who her sons needed in their lives. However, if she'd been choosing a mate for Indigo she would have chosen Thomas Brewster, and she would have been wrong again. Indigo needed someone with as much fire and passion as she had.

"I've been meaning to invite you to go home with me for the winter. You said you'd never traveled, and I'd love to take you to Texas for a few months. You could return in the spring. I'd send Brendon or Nicholas to escort you, and then Flannon would have someone to keep him company on the trip back to Texas," she said.

Laura's first thought was that she couldn't leave Indigo in her time of need. If it weren't for that, she'd go in a heartbeat. Just pack up a trunk and go with Patrick and Mary Margaret. "I couldn't . . ." she mumbled, wishing things had gone differently that day so that she could truly answer yes, yes, yes, because Laura wanted to travel. She wanted to see Texas, where Monroe's wife came from, where Ellie's husband had lived.

"Why?" Monroe asked.

"Yes, Momma, why? We can take care of Indigo or, rather, watch her take care of herself," Reed said.

"You handled the whole place while we were at war. Let us take over and you go with Mary Margaret and Patrick," Rueben said. "Indigo will work this through with or without you here. Lots and lots of hard work will be going on all winter. Houses being built. Babies to tend to. Horses to take care of. A valley to keep under control. We can do it amongst all of us. You did it while we were gone. We'll keep an eye on her, we promise."

"But there weren't babies," Laura laughed.

"Oh, I don't know," Ellie touched her shoulder. "Sometimes I was a big baby even if I was grown. I think you should go. We'll all manage, and the trip will do you good."

"So what do you say, Miz Laura?" Patrick asked. It

would be a blessing to have Laura there with his mother. They could keep each other company.

"I think the answer is yes, and I'm going upstairs to pack a trunk," Laura said. "Indigo will pitch a fit."

"Yes, she will," Geneva said. "Like he said, there's lots of hard work around here. Enough, I reckon for her to get over that, too. Want some help?"

"I'd love some help. But, oh, no, the babies! What if they grow up before I get back?" Laura said.

"I'm sure they won't be ready to break horses before they're even a year old," Douglass said lightly. "I'll put the wedding dress in my room and be over to help you get things packed too. Coming, Adelida?"

"Wouldn't miss it for the world," Adelida said.

"I'll have to go tell Indigo," Laura said forlornly.

"I'll do it," Flannon said from the doorway, where he'd been leaning ever since he'd brought Indigo home. "She's not going to like it one bit, but she doesn't like me, so if she feels like shooting the messenger, at least it won't be one of you."

"Thanks, Flannon," Laura said. "But remember Indigo's first impressions aren't always right."

"This time they are, ma'am," he tipped his hat in her direction. "I wouldn't want them to change. Matter of fact, if they started to change, then I'd be a whole lot more scared than I am with knowing where I stand with that sharp tongue of hers."

"I'm going to be the general of this army of men left behind," Ellie said. "And we're going to put away enough food to feed the thrashers. I can't bear to give that cake to the hogs, though. So I'm going to take the tiers apart, remove the decoration, and put it in the well house to keep cool. Indigo won't even recognize the slices as wedding cake when we serve it tomorrow and Monday. The rest of you men folks can carry trays of food to the well house and be thankful it's not as hot as it could be in August. It should keep until we can eat most of it."

Sweat poured off Indigo as she loaded the wheelbarrow with dirty hay from the horse stalls. First she'd lead a horse out, tether it to the side of the barn, and then go to work. By the time she finished, each stall was so clean even her fastidious mother, Laura, could have poured a cup of stew on the hardened dirt floor and not be afraid to eat it. Her mind, though, was a complete jumble. This morning she was going to marry Thomas Brewster, her childhood friend, and live happily ever after. A week-long honeymoon in Philadelphia. Perhaps a play or an opera. Sightseeing. Being newlyweds. They'd planned to come home to live in the Brewster home in Shirleysburg until Tommy found a farm to buy. Her whole future was planned out. Then it shattered in the space of two minutes. The stars in his eyes when he saw her in all her wedding finery had died instantly when he saw his wife standing in the glowing sunlight. Indigo searched her heart diligently. Had she really loved Thomas as much as she should have on their wedding day, it would have devastated her to see him walk out of the church with that little redhead. But instead it enraged her. Did that mean she didn't love him, but was marrying him because he was Yankee and available?

She slid the flat-nosed shovel under another bunch of manure and soiled straw, scooping it up and over into the wheelbarrow. She wiped sweat from under her nose onto the shoulder of her shirt and went back for another shovel full of pure smelly muck. If hard work solved problems, then by night she should have all the answers to the questions tormenting her soul. She turned to toss the muck into the barrow and there was Flannon chewing on a straw, leaning on an already cleaned stall door, petting a horse.

"What are you doing here? Did you come to gloat? Go away."

"No, I came to bring some news," he said. Indigo had been a vision in that white fluffy dress and veil, that was for sure. But she appealed to him far more in her trousers, at least a couple of sizes too big, and roped in with a belt, the back side bunching up over her tiny waistline and hips. Not that he'd ever let her know that, since he had no intentions of ever forming any kind of a friendship with the woman. He'd rather be friends with Lucifer himself.

"What news did you bring? That the lovely Maudie is staying on in Shirleysburg and they are making a happy little home with their son? God almighty, I shall never be able to show my face in town again."

"Why's that?"

"Because of the sickening pity of all the women. They'll be nice to Maudie Brewster because she's tiny and sweet-looking and has a little baby boy who did without a father for more than a year. But they'll pity me enough to make me gag to death," she said, wishing she could toss a shovel full of soupy manure on Flannon's good Sunday suit and those fancy tooled boots he and Colum were so fond of wearing.

"You're tough. You can stand it and besides, if you become a hermit, you'll never meet another man. Maybe you can marry Charlie Brewster and still get the Brewster name, and then Tommy can be your brother."

She pointed the empty shovel at him, chest level. "Don't you tease me today, Flannon Sullivan. Don't you even think about it. If I want to be a hermit I can, and there's not a darn thing you can do about it."

"Such language from a prissy little bride!" Flannon threw his hand over his chest in mock shock.

"I'm not a bride. Remember, my groom is already married. I'm not little. I'm every bit as tall as you are. And the day Indigo Hamilton was accused of being prissy hasn't dawned yet. Now what news did you come out here to tell me? It had better be good or I might take this shovel and beat the messenger just to make me feel better," she growled.

"Your Momma is going home with my Momma to Texas for the winter. Momma asked Miz Laura, and your brothers all said it would do her good. They said that she'd managed this place while they were off to war and she should have a bit of travel. So anyway, that's the news. She's upstairs packing right now. Patrick is escorting the two ladies to Texas until spring. Then either my brother, Brendon, or Nicholas is going to escort her back and be company for me on the trip home," he said.

"You're lying to me." Indigo backed up to the stall door to keep from falling flat on her bottom. "Besides, Ellie and I helped hold down this place during the war. We worked just as hard as Momma and if anyone deserves to run away to Texas, it's me. So if Momma's going to Texas, so am I." She threw the shovel in the wheelbarrow and started for the house.

Flannon reached out, grabbed her arm, and spun her around to face him. "You don't need to run away, Indigo. Like I told you earlier, you didn't do one thing wrong today. But you do need to stay here and face your demons, not run from them. If you are a proper adult and you love your Momma, you won't go in there all half-cocked, demanding that she take you along just so you can run from Tommy Brewster and his new wife. You'll tell her that you can take care of your own problems and to go on and have a nice trip. Besides, if you did go, when you came back from Texas, Tommy and Maudie Brewster would still be there for you to face. Best to get it over with, once and for all."

"You don't know what is good for me, so shut your mouth." Indigo jerked free of him and stormed toward the house. The closer she got, the heavier the feeling weighed in her chest. Flannon was right, and it sure pricked her soul to have to admit it. Her mother did deserve a few months away from Love's Valley. Goodness only knew she'd never, ever had such an opportunity before. She'd married Harrison Hamilton back when she was a young woman and he'd brought her from Shade Valley to Love's Valley to live in the same house with his mother until Granny Hamilton died. A woman who'd never forgiven her son for marrying beneath him, and who never let Laura forget that she'd married a man superior to her in wealth. As far as Indigo knew, Laura Hamilton had never been outside Huntingdon County, Pennsylvania. But then, neither had Indigo. Today was to be her honeymoon trip all the way to Philadelphia. Just because she couldn't go didn't mean she had to be hateful and force her mother to stay home out of guilt.

She marched under trees decorated with tulle bows, past tables laid out with the finest linen tablecloths and silver trays just waiting to be filled with mountains of food for the wedding guests. She found all three of her brothers and Colum in the kitchen bowing beneath Ellie's commands, running like ants to and fro from the well house, saving food to be used to feed the hired help. She gave them each a brief nod as she stomped up the stairs.

"Uh, oh," Ellie said, hearing the blows of boots on the steps. "I wonder if Flannon is alive or if she did indeed kill the messenger."

"Let's hope not. Flannon is Momma's baby boy. If she's harmed a hair on his pretty little head, she'll have to take it up with Momma. And I wouldn't want to be in her shoes if that's happened." Colum chuckled.

"Momma." Indigo stopped in her mother's doorway. All three of her sisters-in-law looked up from behind the bed where they were sorting things to pack.

"Yes, Indigo. Did Flannon tell you my plans?" Laura asked, searching her daughter's dirty face for some sign of how she'd taken the news.

"He did, and I've come to help with the packing. I'll go get cleaned up first, but I wanted to see if someone has moved that abominable dress out of my room before I go in there. I see Ellie has things under control down in the kitchen," she said.

"The dress is gone." Douglass all but breathed a sigh of relief. She'd been afraid Laura would change her mind if Indigo begged her to stay.

"Then I'll be right back. And Momma, don't worry about me. I'll be fine. I'm mad as a wet hen in a raging thunderstorm right now, but it will pass if I keep busy. I'm not a child. I'm a grown woman of nineteen. An old maid nearly and may truly be one before I trust another man."

"Who are you trying to convince, child? Me or you?" Laura asked. "I know you are a strong woman or I wouldn't leave you at this horrible time. But I've got to admit I'm glad to be going. Just thinking about all that pity every time I went into Shirleysburg these next few months is enough to make me gag."

"Exactly what I told Flannon. Lord, I can just see Mable's face now all squenched up as she dabs her eyes with one of them lacy hankies. 'Poor, poor Indigo and just think of her poor mother. All that expense on the wedding just gone up in smoke. If I can be of any help to you poor, poor Hamiltons, just let me know.' I won't even mention Ida Belle's pity or Mae Ruth's whimpering," Indigo said.

Geneva chuckled. "We better tell the men folks to hide the guns."

"I've got my own, thank you very much, and if I wanted them dead they wouldn't have a chance. I'm a good shot," Indigo declared. "Douglass or Mary Margaret should be able to tell you what-all you'll need. I don't expect you'll need your heavy winter coat since Texas doesn't get much snow." Indigo propped her fists on her hips.

"I guess not." Laura crossed the room and hugged her daughter closely. "Indigo, I really thought Thomas was the man for you, but I figured wrong. You'll find someone who'll make you happy."

"Well, I hope it's not anytime soon. I'm sick of men right now." Indigo hugged her mother back, savoring the smell of the rose soap they made every summer.

Geneva giggled. "I think I remember saying those same words not so long ago."

"Me too," Adelida said.

"And me." Douglass nodded.

"Difference is you said them, and I mean them," Indigo said as she flounced off to her room.

Chapter Three

Flannon leaned the back two rungs of the chair against the bunkhouse wall and propped his feet on the railing. Leaves had begun to turn and fall that week. The old-timers around the feed mill and the general store in Shirleysburg had said there was a hard, long winter in the making. That's exactly what he didn't want to hear, since he'd be stuck in Love's Valley until spring. Wading hip deep snow wasn't something he looked forward to. He hoped Ellie and Colum's house would at least have all the outer walls up and he'd have a nice dry place to work inside through the bitter cold months. For now, though, he tipped his hat forward, the warm autumn sun rays falling on the lower half of his face as his heavy eyelids drooped in preparation for a Sunday afternoon nap.

Indigo had lived through eight whole days. Of course, her survival had been right in her own valley. She had even begged off going to church the past two Sundays, knowing fully well the Brewster family along with the newest member, Mrs. Maudie Brewster, would be there sitting right across from the Hamilton family pew. None of the family said a word that first Sunday since it was the very next day after the wedding fiasco. All of them avoided the subject except Ellie, who'd told her in private that Thomas was there with his wife and son, and everyone had been very nice to them. She'd also said that Thomas looked very happy and that Indigo was wise in letting it all go. Indigo had expected Ellie to be honest, and she'd been prepared for the news. What she hadn't been prepared for was her own I-don't-really-care attitude. She should have been weeping and overcome with grief over her one-and-only love of her life leaving her at the altar, especially forsaking her for another woman, but Indigo felt none of those things. It wasn't grief keeping her in Love's Valley that week. It was simply the idea of not facing those pitying eyes.

Had she truly let it all go in the matter of eight days? Had she been saved in the midnight hour from a marriage that would have been so much less than any one of her brother's happy lives? She didn't have the answers to the questions. Not yet, but she would, and she'd go to church and to town when she was good and ready. Not when any member of the family thought she should—most especially Flannon, who was sitting on the bunkhouse porch. He'd raised an eyebrow that morning at the breakfast table when she said she'd stay home and have lunch ready when they returned from Sunday morning Mass. She'd been fully prepared for a speech, but he'd kept his mouth shut. Not that she'd have cared if he'd started an argument. She could have taken him on and won, she was sure. Her kind had whipped the South once. One little old Rebel didn't look so tough when she was this angry.

She paced the bedroom a while, making a circle, looking out the window each time she came to it. Everyone was having an afternoon nap except her. She wondered where her mother was on the trip to Texas. She wondered if Maudie Brewster had made dinner for the family before she went to Mass. She wondered if Flannon would fall out of the chair before he awoke. Nothing soothed the antsy feeling in the pit of her soul.

Not pacing. Not wondering. Not swearing to the woman in the mirror.

The only thing that brought any kind of relief the past week was a good rousing argument with Flannon. She'd transferred most of the anger she'd had toward Thomas right over to Flannon, and there was nothing she liked better than telling him where he could go and how to get there. It certainly wasn't a place that sported white fluffy clouds and angels with harps either.

Finally, she decided to do something constructive. Make a cake, or two or three or four. The hired hands who came to work on the farm everyday from Shirleysburg and the surrounding area would appreciate it come tomorrow at lunch, and it would keep her hands busy. What she really should do was don her trousers and work clothing and go muck out stalls. But that seemed like even more work than baking, and it was Sunday, the designated day of rest. One shouldn't tempt fate.

She found Geneva in the kitchen, having a cup of tea. "Thought you were napping," she said reaching for an apron from the line of hooks behind the back door. "I've got to do something or my thoughts are going to drive me mad. Figured I'd whip up a few cakes for lunch tomorrow. If we keep those men fed, maybe they'll finish the house building sooner than expected. That way they'll all go home and stop looking at me as if I have sprouted horns or an extra eye."

"I'd like to be napping," Geneva said honestly. "But Reed is snoring and there isn't any sleep for anyone in the room with him, except Angelina. She acts like he's singing lullabies when he snores and snuggles down deeper into the cradle. I'll help you. What kind should we make? Spice cake goes well this time of year, with burnt sugar frosting."

"That's fine. How about a couple of them and a fresh apple one without icing?" Indigo pulled down her mother's recipe book.

"Flour, sugar, cinnamon, ginger." Geneva opened the pantry door and began taking the ingredients out, setting them on the work table.

"Eggs." Indigo read the recipe. If she'd had her way, she wouldn't be making cakes with Geneva. Of all the sisters-in-law, she liked Geneva least. The woman had taken her last brother, the one she'd had hopes would marry a Northern woman. But Indigo didn't figure she had to like the woman to make cakes with her. Reed did seem happy as a piglet in a fresh wallow. Besides, who was Indigo to be making rash judgments against any of the Southern sisters-in-law? After all, she'd been the one hell-bent on having a Northern husband, and look where it got her. Not that she'd ever let such a thing escape from her thoughts into an out-loud statement. They'd never hear it from her lips. She might have to work with them, but she sure didn't have to become bosom buddies with them. She'd still like to cut Tommy's head off and put it on a spike in the church yard, and maybe Flannon's too, just for sitting out there taking an afternoon nap. Flannon would be a thorn in her side all winter. Tommy was worse. He'd promised to love her forever and broken that vow like it was nothing more than crispy pie crust, which set her to thinking about pies also.

"Guess I'd better go to the hen house. I used up the last of what we had gathered this morning for breakfast. Maybe once the cakes are done and cooling, if we've still got time before supper, we'll make a couple of apple pies too."

"Big ones with cinnamon and sugar on the top. I'll go with you to the hen house." Geneva grabbed her bonnet and had the strings tied before Indigo could even find her own faded blue bonnet behind the door hanging among the aprons.

The man had been sitting at the foot of the mountain since daybreak. He'd seen three rigs take the family to what he supposed was church services since it was Sunday morning. She'd been among them. He could tell it was the woman because she was taller than any of the others. Two of the ladies were very small, then there was one who was almost as tall as Geneva Garner, now Hamilton.

Oh, yes, he'd followed Reed and her from Washington all the way to Love's Valley when he'd escaped from jail. She would be dead before he went back to Savannah. He'd set out to do a job and he'd do it. No one would ever say

Jack Dally didn't deliver what he'd promised. He'd promised the sheriff of Savannah, who was his boss in the Klan as well, that Geneva would be dead. So she would be.

Geneva's first husband, Hiriam, had married her because he won her in a card game. Being a tinker, she surely did not fit in with the polite Southern society in Savannah, even if it was in tatters right after the war. She had degraded her position as Hiriam's wife and went right into those ex-slaves' homes to serve food and socialize with them after the Klan had hung one of the slaves. When the Klan went to hang her, Hiriam hid her. He died for it. They burned his home to the ground, and the sheriff was looking at buying the land for taxes. Geneva and the brat she had birthed had to be dead for that to happen.

He'd thought he'd had the job done back in Lynchburg. He had to admit the woman was wily, outsmarting him by smearing jelly all over a dress form and putting it in the bed where she was supposed to be sleeping. He'd stabbed what he thought was her and wiped what he thought was her blood on the curtain when he left the room. A few hours later, he was sitting in jail for attempted murder. By nightfall he was chained to a seat in a rail car on the way to Washington where the president of the United States had men who wanted to interrogate him. They'd never gotten that privilege because he'd escaped before they asked him the first question. Not that he would have given them a bit of information anyway. If he had, the Klan would have made sure he would never tell another thing.

He shifted his position against the tree. Geneva might stay in the house all day, but she'd come out sometime.

Alone. He'd eventually get a good shot at her. He was an expert marksman and a patient man. One bullet straight into the heart and she'd fall like the big horse of a woman she was. It would be an easy matter to come back another day and take care of the kid. That would make the sheriff in Savannah very happy. He'd just mail the paper with the news to the sheriff and be on his way. Maybe to California. The world was at his beck and call when he'd finished his obligation.

"Darn dame anyway," he fretted under his breath. "If Hiriam hadn't come toting her home, we wouldn't have this little problem. But oh no, he had to bring a tinker's daughter to his plantation. Then he didn't even try to control her. Let her go right down amongst those slave people like she was one of them. That got him a hangman's noose for sure. The Klan put out the word that Geneva had done the deed, but that blasted Hamilton got her a pardon from the president. So now it's just a matter of honor."

He stopped and squinted. The back door of the house swung open, and sure enough there was Geneva with another woman. One not nearly as tall, even if she wasn't one of the little women he'd seen going to church that morning. If there was a God in Heaven, he had just blessed Jack with the perfect opportunity. He wet his forefinger and tested the air. No wind. The bullet should travel true. He chose one from his jacket pocket, dipped it in a fresh pile of horse dung, and loaded it into his rifle. Sighting down the barrel, he breathed deeply, waited for the right moment, and pulled the trigger.

"I think I just heard Angelina cry," Geneva turned quickly to go back to the house and tripped over her skirt, falling backward in the grass and hearing the report of a rifle nearby at the same time.

"Oh, my!" Indigo exclaimed, whipping around to see what had happened. Her body turned. Her ankle didn't, and a sharp pain sent her tumbling. But not before the bullet intended for Geneva ripped a four-inch gash from behind her left ear to her forehead. The pain in her foot was nothing compared to the stinging sensation in her hair. Stars appeared in the darkening afternoon sky as she fell back onto Geneva, and then there was nothing but blackness.

The sharp crack of rifle fire brought Flannon out of a doze and into a sitting position. The front legs of the chair cracked as loudly as the gun. His eyes were blurry for a split second before he realized Geneva and Indigo were lying on the ground not ten feet in front of him and there was blood everywhere.

Jack Dally grinned. So he'd gotten two with one shot. "And honey, that is real blood I'm seeing all over those women. Not jelly. Good-bye, Geneva. You shoulda stayed with the tinkers where you belonged. Can't say I'm sorry about the other one, either. War or not, it was just a worthless Yankee," he muttered while he slipped the rifle back into its sheath on his saddle and led his horse up over the mountain. Tomorrow he'd hear all about the shooting in town. Nothing that happened to the Hamiltons, not even that wedding business, stayed a secret very long.

Geneva was addled when she fell hard on her bottom. She thought she saw the glint of something at the foot of the mountain, something shiny, and then Indigo was falling on top of her, pushing her backward, knocking the wind from her lungs. By the time she could force a breath into her chest, Flannon was there, screaming for Colum and lifting Indigo away from her.

"Geneva, are you hit?" Flannon asked, scooping Indigo up into his arms and heading toward the house with her.

"I don't know," Geneva said honestly. Perhaps the pain in her chest was because of a bullet and not from having the wind knocked from her. She felt her dress front and brought back a hand covered in blood. Everything began to spin and then strong arms picked her up and the wind rushed past her face as Colum carried her toward the house.

"They're dead." Jack stared at the hullabaloo in the yard. "Don't bother with the doctor. Call the undertaker."

"What's going on?" Ellie raced down the stairs. "Oh, my Lord, what has happened?" She flung open the parlor door. "Put Geneva here and Indigo there. Colum, who's hurt the worst?"

"Indigo has a head wound," Flannon said.

"I'm not sure where Geneva is hit," Colum said.

"Geneva!" Reed groaned when he reached the bottom of the staircase. "What's going on? Who shot my wife?"

"We don't know. Appears to have come from the foot of the mountain," Flannon said, laying Indigo on the settee, ripping off his shirt, and putting pressure on the wound with the material. "There was just one shot. I don't think Geneva is hit. I think she got the wind knocked from her when Indigo fell backward on her. Reed, you check your wife. Rueben, you'd better ride for the doctor in a hurry. I'm not sure if Indigo is even alive."

Cold chills covered Rueben's body. Without a word, he kissed Adelida on the forehead, grabbed his hat, and was out the door. Whoever had done this would pay, and if his only sister died because of it, they'd better be on their knees right now making things right with their maker because they were about to have an up-close and personal experience with the Almighty in a hurry.

"Geneva is fine. No wounds." Reed almost wept as he gathered his wife, bloody clothing and all, into his arms. "Indigo? Flannon, is she alive? Who did this?"

"I have no idea who did it, and she has a pulse for now. Looks like it grazed her scalp pretty good. The doctor will have to put a bunch of stitches in it. I'll keep the pressure on it until he gets here."

"Colum, what are you doing?" Ellie asked.

"I'm going hunting. The rest of you stay right here. I work best alone," he said coldly serious and eerily calm. "The track will be fresh, and whoever is out there is not expecting anyone to come looking this quick. Also, he was shooting to kill, so he'll be thinking he's got all the time in the world."

"Be careful," Ellie said with a nod. Colum would take care of it. She had faith in her husband. "Should we take her to her bedroom?" she asked Flannon.

"No, leave her right here," he answered. "The less we move her, the better. One of you women might take off her shoes and stockings and make sure she's not hit anywhere else. I'll keep the pressure on, but I can shut my eyes while you check."

Adelida removed Indigo's shoes while Ellie unbuttoned the dress.

"Oh my, she's got a terrible foot. Not shot, but already turning blue. I'd say she turned her ankle pretty bad. It could be broken. I'll go get a cold compress and keep it on it until the doctor gets here," Adelida said.

"No holes anywhere else, but I'm taking these bloody clothes off, Flannon, and putting a robe on, so keep your eyes averted a while longer. Your shirt is dripping on the floor. Adelida, bring some towels to Flannon. A whole stack of them," Ellie called out.

Flannon handed his shirt over to Adelida when she gave him a bundle of kitchen towels. The gaping wound was still flowing. Indigo's long brown braid was soaked in it. The settee would have to be cleaned soon or the blood would never come out of the floral print covering.

"Head wounds bleed worse than any other kind." He repeated his mother's words he'd heard so often growing up with five brothers who were constantly in trouble of one kind or other. Saints above, but he didn't like Indigo. Couldn't abide being in the same room with her most of the time, but he'd never have wished her dead. Well, almost never.

Douglass and Monroe came wandering lazily in the front door about that time, stopping dead in their tracks when they saw the scene in the parlor. "What . . ." Monroe rushed away from his wife and toward his sister.

"Someone shot her. Don't know if they were out to kill Geneva or if it was Indigo they were after, or if it was some freak accident. Colum has gone to track them. Rueben's gone for the doctor."

"Is she . . . ?" Douglass bit back the words.

"She's alive. Has a pulse and it's pretty good. Adelida says her ankle is in a mess. Looks like she sprained or broke it when she fell on top of Geneva. Geneva is fine.

Wind knocked from her and she's pretty rattled, but she's coming around," Flannon reported.

"I'm not bleeding?" Geneva asked weakly.

"No, you're not hit." Reed let her go enough to look deeply into her eyes. "Geneva, did you see anything? Anything at all?"

"Just a shiny something in the trees, then I tripped on my skirt and fell and it sounded like a rifle fired, and Indigo fell backward on top of me," she said. "Oh no, it couldn't be? Not the Klan?" Her eyes widened.

"Jack Dally. Did you see red boots? He said he'd kill you. I'll send a telegram tomorrow to Washington. Maybe he's escaped."

"Who is Jack Dally, and what's this about red boots?" Flannon asked.

"We'll explain later," Reed said. So much for keeping the secret from his family. He and Geneva had agreed that they'd tell everyone they'd been married a whole year so that Angelina would be legally his child. Now they'd have to know the truth: that Geneva had been married before, that she was widowed, that the Klan had killed her worthless husband. But better secrets be out, and Jack Dally be caught, than his wife dead.

They waited more than a long, exhausting hour before they heard horses coming down the lane in a dead run. Rueben rushed inside, his face drawn and pale with worry, the doctor right on his heels.

"Move over and let me look." Dr. Rushing had his black bag open before Flannon could even take a step backward. "Messy. Needs stitches. Get me some warm water and soap. I'll clean it out with something stronger after that. Then I'll stitch it up. This the only wound? What about Reed's wife?"

"Geneva is fine," Douglass said. "We've sent her upstairs with Reed."

"Indigo's ankle is all swollen and bruised," Adelida said from the end of the settee, where she'd been wringing the cloth in and out of cold water for the past two hours.

"Check that later. It can wait. She's lost a lot of blood. Be weak for days, I'm sure. At least most women would be. Can't say that about Indigo. She's tough as boot leather," Dr. Rushing said as he washed the wound.

"She'll live?" Rueben asked.

"I think so." Dr. Rushing smiled. "Just hope she stays out long enough for me to sew this up. It's going to hurt like hell. Pardon me, ladies. But that's the only way to describe it. I need a razor." He'd begun to cut the hair away from the wound with small, sharp scissors he'd pulled from his kit.

"She's going to have a hissy!" Adelida watched dark tresses land on the floor.

"Maybe so, but we can't have a hair getting in the wound and infecting it," Dr. Rushing said. "Most of this side of her head needs to be shaved to prevent that. Who wants the job? I'll look at her ankle while you get it ready."

"I'll do it." Flannon stepped up. "She already hates me, so it won't matter. She'd never forgive any of you."

"Might as well shave her whole head," Dr. Rushing said. "I'll do the part around the wound. You do the rest. Then all her hair can grow out even. Be easier on her in the long run than having half a head of long hair and baldness on the other."

"Thank goodness she's not awake," Ellie said.

"Amen." Flannon cut off her blood-soaked braid and began the job.

Colum rushed in the back door. "Doc, I found where the shooter had been watching the house. From the cigar butts, I'd say he's been there most of the day waiting. He's leading a horse back down the foot of the mountain toward the upper end of the valley. Staying in the shadows of the trees. I'd say he's on his way to Orbisonia. Horse has a particular hoof pattern, so it shouldn't be hard to find him. But I wanted the doctor to know that he's dipped the bullet in fresh horse manure. There's a pile with a perfect hole in it. Measured it against the spent shell. It fits."

"What does that mean?" Adelida asked.

"Infection if we hadn't known," the doctor said. "I'd say whoever did this intended one or both of these women to be dead from the shot or the infection. I'll leave a stitch out at the backside of the gash. It'll leave a gaping scar but her hair should cover it when it grows back in. More the reason to shave it all off, in case it does infect. We'll have to give it a good cleansing before I stitch and keep a watchful eye on it. Why would anyone want to kill Indigo? Now I could see *her* wanting to shoot Thomas Brewster or even his new wife, but . . ."

"They weren't out to shoot Indigo," Reed said tersely from the bottom of the staircase. "It was Geneva, I'm sure, he was after. I'll tell you all about it. But before I do, Colum and I are going to find this shooter and take care of matters."

"Keep it within the law." The doctor picked up a second razor and began to help Flannon. "Let the law hang him for this."

"What are you doing?" Colum's big brown eyes

widened as he saw Indigo's hair falling in clumps on the parlor floor.

"Shaving her head," the doctor said matter-of-factly. "This man assures me that Indigo hates him already, so he's going to take the blame for the job."

"Saints above, have pity on my poor little brother. She's going to go hunting, and poor old Flannon is going to be in the crosshairs," Colum intoned as he crossed himself and took off out the back door toward the stables where Reed was already saddling his favorite horse.

Chapter Four

Indigo's eyes fluttered. To wake meant facing the pain in her head. The dream slowly faded into a gray fog, and she gave in to reality. She never had headaches in her entire life, and in her half-sleep she'd thought it was all part of the dream. It was a ploy to stay home from church, claiming her head hurt too badly to open her eyes. Slowly she opened them to find Adelida sitting beside the bed, knitting needles in hand with something pale pink falling into her lap. Why was Rueben's wife sitting beside her? She rolled her eyes toward the ceiling, surprised to see she wasn't in her room at all, but in the bunk house.

"Where am I?" she asked, her voice a raspy whisper instead of the demanding tone she wanted.

"Ah, you are awake," Flannon said from the doorway. "We'd wondered if you were going to sleep forever. Guess that medicine the doctor forced down your throat before he left did its job."

"What doctor?" Her voice was a bit stronger but still

hoarse. One drop of moisture remained in her mouth, and it tasted foul. Her head hurt and her foot throbbed. Every muscle in her body weighed a ton. Moving her arm to rub her eyes was a major undertaking.

"You were shot yesterday morning," Adelida put the knitting aside and laid her hand on Indigo's forehead. No fever yet. The doctor said it would come in forty-eight hours if the wound was infected by the tainted bullet.

"Shot?" Indigo reached up to touch her aching head only to find it bandaged completely. Her eyes sought out Flannon's. She didn't like him one bit, the sorry, swaggering, good-looking Rebel. But one thing she could depend on was that he'd tell her the truth. If it was the last thing she wanted to hear, he'd tell her exactly what had happened, and that's the way it was. Every one of those Texans was like that: Douglass; Ellie's husband, Colum; and Flannon. Indigo had always figured Rebels to be liars, but not so with the three her family came carting home after the war. Even Geneva and Adelida could be depended on to tell the truth, but none of them as much as Flannon. He didn't like her, so he didn't even try to spare her feelings when he said what was on his mind.

"It's a long story." Flannon crossed the room to the bedside. "Can you sit up if I prop pillows behind you?"

"Of course, but I don't need your help." Indigo swung her legs over the side of the bed. The room began to turn in slow circles that got faster and faster, then a high-pitched noise set up a howling noise in her ears.

"Whoa!" Flannon grabbed her before she went forward on her face. "You better let me and Adelida help brace you up, and then we'll see how long you can stay awake this first time out of the chute."

"I'm fine. I can stand on my own two feet." She gritted her teeth, not liking the feeling of almost giving in to the vapors or the feeling Flannon's strong arms evoked when he gently laid her back on pillows Adelida fluffed up behind her. Good Lord, she'd been shot. Had Tommy's new little bit of Southern fluff decided to do away with her?

"Sure, you are fine and can do whatever you like in about six weeks. You wouldn't have gotten far if you had tried to stand on your own two feet, lady. Your ankle is so sprained, it's what's going to keep you in this bed for six weeks, not that scratch on your head," Flannon said in his usual slow Texas drawl.

"I'll go get Geneva. She wanted me to come tell her soon as Indigo awoke." Adelida disappeared out the door.

"What am I doing in the bunk house? What do you mean a scratch on my head? I thought I'd been shot in the leg." Indigo hated to depend on Flannon for anything.

"Your foot is badly sprained, like I said. It was my idea to bring you to the bunk house. It'll be a lot easier to get you in and out of a one-floor place than up and down stairs. The scratch on your head is a bad graze, bone deep from a bullet. That's what I meant by the shooter. He tried to shoot Geneva, but funny thing is, she stumbled and fell about the time he shot the rifle. You turned right sharp to see what had happened, twisted your ankle, and almost got killed. If you hadn't whipped around there, the bullet would have gone right into your brain," he explained.

"You are staying in the bunk house?" she asked. Sweet Mary, Mother of Christ, that's all she needed! The hired hands would go back to town and tell everyone she and Flannon were both in the bunk house. Her reputation would be in worse shambles than it was already. Everyone would be saying she'd taken up with a Rebel just to get back at Thomas Brewster. She'd rather die and marry Lucifer.

"Yes, I am. You have this room. I've been told it's the old foreman's private quarters. I've made myself at home right next to the door in the main part of the bunk house. They didn't have the shooter behind bars until this morning when he showed up at the Shirleysburg Hotel. Reed and Colum were right on his tail, and they dragged him down the street and to the sheriff's office, where he'll be staying until the trial. Seems he wasn't out to kill you at all, but Geneva." Flannon pulled up a chair, turned it around backward, straddled it, and leaned his elbows on the back.

"Geneva? Whatever for?" Indigo tried to digest the fact that she'd even been shot. She reached up and touched the bandages again, wondering if they'd washed the blood from her hair or if it was tangled up in a muddled mess under a turban-style bandage.

"Because." Geneva swept into the room and pulled a chair to the bed, touching Indigo's forehead to make double sure she didn't have a fever. "Do you want some more pain medicine? The doctor said you could have a spoonful twice a day once you woke up but not to overdo it."

"Will it make me sleepy and my mouth all dried out?" Indigo asked.

"Yep, it sure will," Flannon chuckled.

"No, I don't want it. I'll live with the headache and the throb in my foot. Don't you laugh at me." She glared at him.

"Yes, ma'am," he drawled.

"I'm so very sorry." Geneva sat down and took Indigo's hand in hers. "This is all my fault, and I wanted to be the one to explain. Reed told the rest of the family, but I have to tell you since you took the bullet intended for me. It all started a little more than a year ago. My father, Daniel O'Grady, was a tinker, and we were living in the slave quarters of a burned-out plantation home. He went into town on Saturday like he always did to bring home supplies. Only one Saturday he brought home Hiriam Garner, a tobacco grower from Savannah. They'd started playing cards in a saloon in town and were still having a good time, drinking and playing, when the place shut down for the night. Daddy invited Hiriam to our place and when he'd lost all his money to the man, he used me for the next round of bets. He lost, and Hiriam won me. Hiriam was nearly fifty and had been looking for a wife to bear him a son to carry on the name." Geneva paused.

If Indigo had felt the least bit drowsy, she was fully awake by the time Geneva got this far with her story. Great glory, Indigo knew she'd been a tinker's daughter and that was bad enough, but to be the pawn in a card game! What exactly had Reed brought home? A divorcee with a baby and, oh dear, Angelina wasn't even Reed's child.

"Are you cold?" Geneva asked.

"No, go on," Indigo said.

"He married me in a church, but it wasn't Catholic. I always felt like I was living in pure sin. Hiriam had an ex-slave named Mazell who came to help with the cleaning. The Klan hanged her husband. Said it was because he looked at a white woman the wrong way, but it was because he was leading the other ex-slaves away from the way the Klan wanted them to vote. Anyway, I went to her house and helped serve the people at the funeral, and the Klan got really mad at me. I think they'd been looking for a reason to kill me for a long time. It didn't matter that I was expecting a baby. I had been consorting with the ex-slaves. That gave them enough reason. So they came to the house and I hid. Hiriam offered to kill me for them, but they said if they couldn't have me, they'd just hang him, and they did. I was hiding in the cellar and saw the whole thing. Then they burned down the house. I took what money Hiriam had hid in the cellar and walked to town. I barely got there in time to catch the next stage. The sheriff, two of his deputies, and the mayor of Savannah were right there asking the ticket taker if I'd been around. I could have reached out from the stage door and slapped any one of them. The ticket taker didn't know me but with all the dirt and grime on me, he would have never recognized me anyway. Your brother, Reed, boarded the same stage. The next morning, the driver of the stage and his shotgun rider robbed it and threw the two of us out in the dirt in the middle of South Carolina swamp country. An old black lady gave us the use of her cabin while she was away, and that night I went into labor. At daybreak, Reed found me in the last stages and delivered Angelina for me. His words when he came in the room were that he didn't know I was about to have a baby, he just thought I was fat." Geneva smiled at the memory.

"In the course of traveling together and all the difficulties we faced, we fell in love and married. The priest put down on the marriage license that we were married the year before so Angelina would truly be a legitimate Hamilton. The deputy who was among those four Klansmen who hanged Hiriam followed us to Lynchburg and tried to kill me there. Reed had him arrested and sent him to Washington so the president could interrogate him, but he escaped. That's who shot you, Indigo. He was trying to shoot me. Remember I thought I heard the baby and turned quickly, got tangled up in my skirt, and fell? That's when you took the bullet intended for me. I'm just so sorry."

"Reed actually told you he thought you were just fat?" Indigo asked incredulously. Surely she'd heard wrong. Reed was the heartthrob of the whole area before he left for the war.

"Yes, he did." Geneva's big crystal-clear, light blue eyes twinkled.

"And you still married him?" Indigo asked. "I'd have sent him packing on the spot."

"Not that day but several weeks later, I'd forgiven him. We both went to confession and got married in Washington on our way here," Geneva said. "But for all legal reasons we've been married a year and Angelina is a Hamilton. Someday maybe we'll tell her. Reed doesn't want to; says she's not born of his flesh, but of his heart. I am truly sorry that you were hurt because of me."

Indigo shook her head. "I don't like you or any of the others, but if you'd been killed, who would have taken care of Angelina? I sure can't nurse her. I was pretty mad when Reed came home dragging another Southern woman into the valley. I'd held out hope I'd have one brother with some sense. Evidently, he'd already lost his mind if he called you fat. It's a wonder you'd even have him after that."

Indigo's voice weakened even as she talked, evidence that just being awake a few minutes had worn her out. Maybe the infection had started in her wound and would go to her brain. Geneva shut her eyes for a second of silent prayer. She'd never forgive herself if she'd brought death to the valley. Even if it was Indigo who would never accept her.

"I do like Angelina, and no one outside the family had better ever say she isn't my niece. I'll fight them and I'll win," Indigo said.

Flannon chuckled deep in his chest. "Not today you won't." If a feather had floated down from the ceiling and touched him, it would have knocked him to the floor, he was so surprised to even see Indigo have an ounce of compassion. He figured she'd awake cussing and swearing, refusing to even speak to Geneva.

"I'll fight *you* any day." Indigo cut her eyes around at Flannon Sullivan. She'd been nice long enough. She still didn't like Flannon and she wasn't going to like him, not today or tomorrow or next week. "And I want you out of the bunk house or else take me back into the main house, right now. I refuse to stay in this place with you. Do you know what people will say? I sure don't want my name linked up with the likes of you."

"Sorry, darlin'," he drawled. "That ain't happenin'. I'm the one who's on duty to keep you alive in case any more of the shooters are lurking around. The ladies will take care of you in the day when I'm working. Can't see what the fuss is. You've got your room. I've got mine. Same as in the big house."

"Don't you dare call me endearments. That's blasphemy coming from your lips. I know how you feel about me because I feel the same about you. And the difference is," Indigo said icily, "there's no one else here and folks will talk."

"Folks are goin' to talk no matter what. Look at Douglass and Monroe. They came all the way across country, just the two of them. And Adelida and Rueben even shared a room on the ship and were stranded on an island without anyone around," he reminded her.

"I'm not them," she said. Fighting with Flannon at least brought back some of the spunk. Things were different with her three brothers and even with Colum and Ellie. Holy smoke, they'd all ended up married, so the time they'd spent together was like dust swept under the rug. No one noticed it. But she wouldn't be marrying Flannon Sullivan, so their close quarters with no chaperones would be hung right out on the gossip line for everyone to see.

"I'm hungry. Geneva, could you find me some food?" she finally said through gritted teeth. Flannon could make her madder than anyone else in the whole world. Thomas Brewster hadn't riled her up when he left her at the altar as much as Flannon did leaning against the door jamb and declaring that she was staying in the bunk house with him. Damn his old Rebel heart anyway. She wished he'd been the one in front of Geneva and taken the bullet. She might have danced at his funeral.

"I'd be glad to." Geneva smiled.

After Geneva left, Indigo narrowed her eyes at Flannon. Her dark eyebrows knit together into a solid line, and her mouth was barely a slash. She lowered her head and glared at him. "I want to go back in the house. They can make me a bed in the parlor. I will not stay out here with you." There were times when she'd need total privacy for necessary things. Granted, the outhouse wasn't that far, but she'd be hanged for a traitor before she asked Flannon to carry her all the way down the path to the hired hands' outhouse. Or to help her up and down on a chamber pot either. The war must have touched his brain as much as it had Reed's if he thought he could really take care of her needs.

"Ain't happening," he said. "The ladies are going to come take care of you during the day. I'll be here at night. Reed will be with Geneva upstairs to protect her and Angelina until the trial is over in a few weeks. This is more right than me sleeping in the same room with you in the house, and that's what I'd have to do to protect you."

"The man is locked up. I don't need protecting," she argued.

"He was locked in chains in a railroad car and he escaped. He's part of the Klan. We don't know who or when they might get a wild hair and try to break him out of jail and bring a full-fledged war to Love's Valley," Flannon said. "I'm leaving as soon as Geneva gets here with your dinner. We're working on Ellie and Colum's house today. You won't have to put up with me very much. I'm just your protector at night so your brothers can spend their nights with their wives and not take turns out here seeing that you aren't shot again. For once in your spoiled little life, you don't get your way."

"How bad is what's under the bandage?" She changed the subject. She'd get Reed to take her back in the house later in the afternoon. He couldn't refuse her anything, and he'd be feeling the guiltiest because his wife should have been shot. Flannon would learn who had the most clout in the Hamilton family. Blood was thicker than water, and she would have her way. He could write it in stone and put it on the front porch. She wasn't spending one night in the bunk house with a Rebel.

"Just about as bad as a graze can get. You lost a lot of

blood. There's a bunch of stitches. They start behind your ear. There's a bit that won't be covered by your hair on your forehead, but Doc was careful to stitch it right close so the scar shouldn't be too bad. He left out one stitch at the very back so it could drain out infection. It's way back in your hair so it won't even show here in a few months," Flannon explained.

"Infection?" She frowned.

"Jack Dally is the shooter's name. He dipped the bullet that cut a path across your skull in a fresh horse manure pile before he loaded it. Old trick to bring infection to the victim in case the bullet don't kill them outright. Colum is the tracker in our family. He went right away and found where Dally had been waiting all day. Found the spent shell and the manure. Came right back before he even went to find the man to let the doctor know what he might be dealin' with. That's when he decided to leave one stitch out. It's a gaping hole but your hair will cover it," Flannon said.

"My hair? Did they have to cut it away from the wound?" she asked then held her breath. A gaping wound. A scar from above her ear to her forehead. She'd be a fright for months and months.

Flannon grimaced. Now why couldn't Geneva hurry up with that food and answer that question? But like he'd told them twice already—once when he offered to carry the message to the barn and tell her that her mother was going to Texas; the other when he picked up the scissors and straight razor to help the doctor—she already hated him so what difference did it make?

"We had to shave your head," he said bluntly, not trying to sugarcoat the issue. "Doc said even one stray hair getting in your wound could be fatal."

"You shaved my head?" Her eyes were suddenly bigger than a dinner plate. "You let them shave my head? I'm bald under this? My hair is gone? It's never had scissors put to it. We braid it and burn the ends when they get frayed. You didn't really let them shave my head?"

"They had nothing to do with it. Doc and I did it," he said. "We worked together to make sure it was all done proper. He said half of your head had to be done anyway, and it would be crazy looking to have one side all long and the other trying to catch up. So yes, you are bald."

"Go away," she huffed. "Get out of my sight. I absolutely despise you and I never want to see you again. Go back to Texas. I'll pay for another whole work crew out of my own money just to be rid of you."

"Dinner is served," Geneva said brightly from the doorway.

"Not a minute too soon." Flannon escaped so fast he almost knocked Geneva down.

"He shaved my head. That sorry Rebel shaved my head. Now I'm worse than just a jilted bride. I'm the jilted bald bride. I think I hate him more than anything or anyone in this world."

"He said he'd help the doctor because you already didn't like him," Geneva said.

"He was stone cold right about that. If I can't go to the house until this Jack Dally is hung or safely sent back to the president, then I want a pair of crutches made. Not only am I hungry, it's been a long time since I've been to the outhouse and I need to go. You can help me hobble out there this time, but I can't ask Flannon to do such a thing. And hand me a fork. I'm so hungry and so mad I could eat . . . wedding cake." She stiffened her resolve. She'd get over it, she vowed. At least as long as she was laid up with a bad ankle and was bald, no one would expect her to go to church or to town.

Reprieve from pity had been given even if it was a heck of a way to get it.

Chapter Five

Indigo made it from the edge of the bed to the makeshift privy Ellie had prepared for her. Back when Ellie was a captive in a trapper's cabin and nearly died, Colum had built her such a room where there was a bottomless chair with the chamber pot under it. Worked right well, as did the crutches. But it still scalded Indigo to think that her crutches and the necessary room were products of a Texan's ingenuity.

Pulling up her drawers was no easy feat, standing on one foot and holding the other up. Even that amount of independence fed her soul. She picked up her crutches and clomped over to the shaving mirror hanging on the wall. Dark circles still ringed her eyes, but they weren't as ugly as they'd been two days before when she awoke from a drug-induced sleep.

Today she was going out on the bunk house porch and they were bringing her something to do. She'd do anything to pass time and beat boredom. She didn't care if it was hemming tea towels, and she disliked any chore that had to do with holding a needle. Two days of lying in bed and being waited on like an invalid was as bad as the pity she'd shunned from the people in Shirleysburg. She shed everything she wore, soaped up the washcloth hanging on the wash stand, and gave herself a bath. She would have loved to sink down in the bathtub hanging on the back porch, into steaming hot water, staying there until all the warmth had escaped. That wouldn't be happening for a long, long time. Not until her foot was totally healed.

She donned the clean underthings Adelida had lain on the chair next to the wash stand and shoved aside the white lawn nightrail. She wasn't wearing a gown and robe outside. She reached for the day dress of faded blue-and-white checks hanging on a nail and carefully buttoned it all the way up the front. By the time she hobbled back to the bed, she was exhausted but refused to fall back into the beckoning sheets and pillows. She determined that she'd stay up all day and not set foot back into the bedroom until night. With that decided, she sat down long enough to put one work boot on, picked up the chamber pot on her way out of the room and carried it all the way down the back path to the outhouse on her own. It had been embarrassing the past two days when Ellie had to take care of that business, but she wouldn't have to do it again. As of today, Indigo Hamilton wasn't depending on anyone for anything.

If they'd just bring her a Colt revolver she wouldn't even need Flannon to stay in the bunk house at night. She was an excellent shot. Too bad she hadn't seen the fool hiding back in those woods like a coward, shooting at unarmed women. If she had, he wouldn't be in jail; he'd be pushing up weeds in the cemetery. Entertaining herself with that vision, she slowly made her way back into the bunk house where she rinsed the chamber pot with the bath water from the basin, amazed that she could get the job done standing on one foot. It proved a strong woman couldn't be held down with something as simple as a sore foot.

When she finished that job, she was ready to go outside. She reached to push the front door open at the same time Flannon threw it open from the other side, almost knocking her backward.

"What in the world are you doing out of bed?" he asked abruptly. Things had gone fairly smooth the past two days. He worked from daybreak until past dark, coming in bone tired to clean up and sleep, only to start all over again. Scarcely a dozen words had been exchanged with the patient behind the closed foreman's bunk house door. It was perfect, and now she'd gotten up, dressed, and the whole nine yards. Perfection had ended.

"I'm not dying," she declared. "If I lay in there with nothing to do for another day, I'll be ready for a strait-jacket. Now get out of my way. I'm going to sit on the porch and talk Adelida into bringing me a bushel of beans to shell this morning. By afternoon I may be ready to tackle those steps up to the kitchen door and make a pie."

"The doctor said . . ." Flannon started to argue.

"The doctor can talk until he's blue. I'm tired of the bed and I'm not an invalid. My foot is sprained. I've got crutches which you made so you know very well they'll hold me up. My head doesn't hurt today. Pulls like it's healing and I'm sure under the bandages is a fright that will scare the pure devil out of me, but right now, this minute, I'm going outside. So get out of my way, Flannon Sullivan."

"Nothing could scare the devil out of you," Flannon stood aside. Like the doctor said, Indigo was made of tough old bull hide. She might look all frail in that faded dress and her head wrapped up like a mummy, but she was made of steel and heaven help anyone who got in her way. All he'd promised was to spend his nights in the bunk house keeping one eye open and both ears tuned to the dangers outside, protecting the ice queen of the north. He hadn't promised to keep her in the bedroom, or to cater to her every whim. If she wanted to sit on the porch and shell beans all day, then she could do just that. Her brothers could deal with her.

"Don't you talk to me like that. You may be Douglass' brother but you're not mine. In my eyes you're just hired help," she said. Who would have ever thought she'd be relying on a Rebel, one that was half Irish and half Mexican at that, to keep her safe.

Flannon's jaws worked in anger. He wouldn't have been confined to that bed even for two days. He'd have been up and finding something to do the moment he awoke. He didn't even glance at her trying to get situated in the rocking chair on the wide porch, but he was certainly aware that she was there. Going back to the house he was helping build for Colum and Ellie, he tried to sort through his feelings, but it was useless. That he wasn't pleased with Indigo being out of bed and in his sight more shouldn't be any surprise. All they did was rub each other the wrong way.

"Hey, Colum, Indigo got up and is sitting on the porch. Says she's going to shell beans," he told his brother when he reached the construction site.

"Oh, dear," Ellie exclaimed from behind a wall. "I better go see what's going on. I'd hoped she'd stay put a few days but that would be asking for a miracle. Is she . . ."

"No, she's not a bit nice. She's snippy," Flannon answered the unspoken question. He wondered why on earth everyone had catered to Indigo her whole life. Then a niggling little voice down deep inside his heart reminded him that Douglass was the youngest child, the only girl after six sons, and she'd been even more spoiled than Indigo.

"Well, then I'll get on back to the house and help keep her busy today. Adelida and I were talking about picking beans and canning them today. I guess she overheard that yesterday. She never has been one to like being sick." Ellie brushed a kiss across Colum's cheek, picked up her skirt, and gingerly picked her way around the piles of lumber.

"Good woman," Flannon said.

"Which one? Ellie? Or Indigo?"

"Good Lord, that question doesn't even bear answering," Flannon snapped. "Ellie is wonderful. Indigo is a handful of pure evil."

"Time was when I thought the same of Ellie. She's the one who gave me this scar if you'll remember." Colum pointed to the faint white line on his cheek.

"Yes, but she's changed. Indigo won't and never will. Remember what Grandfather Montoya said. Some women were born evil and get worse as they grow up," Flannon reminded him.

"Guess so." Colum grinned. Come spring when Flannon had spent a winter in Love's Valley, he wouldn't be a bit surprised if lots of things had changed. They had sure done so the previous spring when he was all ready to get out of

Love's Valley. Now a team of wild horses couldn't take him back to Texas permanently. Life was here with Ellie. Love was here with Ellie. Wherever she was, there lay Colum's heart and he couldn't fathom living without her.

"What are you doing out here?" Ellie rounded the end of the bunk house to find Indigo settled into a rocking chair with her sore leg propped up on the bottom rung of the porch railing.

"Getting some fresh air. Keeping from going crazy. Where're the beans? And don't bring me a tea towel or handwork to keep me busy. If you'll remember, I've spent the last year doing handwork for my new home. Every time I pick up a needle I think about that woman in the doorway of the church."

"I thought we weren't going to ever mention that again." Ellie swept her long skirt to the side and sat down on the porch.

"We weren't, but shoving dirt under the rug doesn't mean it's not there or that it's not still dirt," she said. "The air is wonderful this morning, Ellie. Fall is on the way for sure. Just think a year ago, it was just me and you and Mother. Now the valley is filling up. Next fall Angelina and Ford will be walking and squealing. Before long the whole valley will be alive with kids and giggles again. That should take away some of the sting of the war, don't you think?"

"Philosopher this morning, are you?" Ellie smiled, keeping her own secret safe a few more days. She and Colum would tell the family in a few weeks. Right now they needed to concentrate on Geneva and Indigo, to get the horrid man responsible for the shooting brought to trial and punished.

"Had a lot of time to think in that bed the past two days. I can't remember when I've been laid up that long.

Must've been when I was a little girl and got the measles. Momma made me stay in a dark room for ten days. I thought the world had come to an end," Indigo said.

"So are you still mad at Flannon for shaving your head?" Ellie asked, biting her tongue to keep back the laughter.

"Hate that egotistical man. Absolutely hate him, Ellie. He's so smug and self-righteous and thinks he's always right. He didn't get a single one of Colum's good qualities." Indigo rolled her eyes heavenward. Even the mention of Flannon set her mood on edge.

"I hated Colum too, remember. An Irishman with an attitude. A Mexican with a big ego. A Rebel to boot. Who'd ever thought I'd end up in love with him? Did I just hear you say a kind word about Colum?" Ellie said.

"Yes, you did. I can see good things when they are there. I'll never be happy that you married a Rebel. I would have never believed it of you. Or that my three brothers would wind up with Southern women and big stories to tell about how they got them. But that's where it ends, Ellie, so don't be going getting stars in your eyes and trying to match me up with Flannon just because I said I despise him. Oh, don't think I can't see what you're doing. I'm injured but I'm not blind. I won't ever fall for that man. Not ever. He's the devil incarnate."

"Hello, Indigo," Thomas Brewster said, driving a wagon pulled by a team of four horses around the house and toward the site where Ellie and Colum were building their home.

"Thomas?" Indigo could scarcely believe her eyes. Did her ex-groom actually have the nerve to set foot on Hamilton property?

"I'm going to the garden to see if Geneva and Adelida have started picking beans," Ellie escaped.

"Traitor," Indigo mumbled under her breath.

Thomas hopped down from the wagon and sat down in almost the same spot as Ellie had vacated. "I've been meaning to talk to you, Indigo."

"What's there to talk about? It seems like it's too late for that."

"I suppose it is. I know I gave you my promise to love you and take care of you. But I honestly thought Maudie was dead," he said.

"Thomas, you never even mentioned her to me. You never told me you'd married another woman down there in the South."

"I know. Like I said on that day in church, it was too painful to talk about. I just loved her so much, and then she was dead, or so I thought. I just wanted to apologize to you. I owe you that much."

"What would you have done, Thomas, if it had been a man standing in that doorway telling everyone that he was my husband?" Indigo asked. To be sitting there in her worst day dress, her head in bandages, her bare foot shining in all its purple and yellow glory. To know that Maudie—pretty, petite Maudie with her glorious red hair and delicate features—was home fixing dinner for Thomas while she laughed at the antics of their son. It was almost more than a woman should have to bear.

"I wouldn't know since it didn't happen. I would hope I would be man enough to step aside and forgive you for breaking your promise to love me forever," he said.

"I had no choice but to step aside. I'm not sure I'll ever be able to believe in promises again, though. Did you ever really love me, Thomas?"

"I thought I did. I thought I could be happy with you

here in the world we are used to. But Maudie brings more than happiness to me. She's my world, Indigo. I shouldn't even be telling you this, but she holds my heart in her hands. I'd die for her," Thomas said.

"And you wouldn't have done that for me?"

Thomas answered truthfully. "You would have been a good wife and mother even if you do have a temper that would take some getting used to. I would have been content to live with you the rest of my life, and we might have learned to be compatible. But the spark wasn't there Indigo, not like it is with Maudie. The fire wasn't there. I'm not saying you won't have it with someone someday. I hope you do. But we didn't have it."

Indigo was speechless.

"I'll go now. I just wanted to apologize and ask for your forgiveness. Someday maybe you'll be over the hurt and can give that to me. I'm very happy and Maudie is staying in Shirleysburg. We're buying the Tennison farm out toward Orbisonia. There's a couple of women in the church who've offered to pack up the things you brought to our house and bring them back to you," he said.

Indigo nodded. "Keep them. Give them away. Burn them. I never want to see them again."

"Good day then." Thomas tipped his hat and crawled back up on the seat of the wagon. "I'll be seeing you. And I'm sorry you got shot. I hope you recover well."

"Just go," she mumbled through clenched teeth. To think that a purebred Huntingdon County man could rile her more than a Rebel was enough to boggle the brain.

So the fire hadn't been there with her, had it? Sparks didn't fly between them. She tilted her head back to keep the tears at bay. She wasn't going to cry for Thomas and what might have been. According to him it would have been nothing more than a contented existence. In all honesty, she didn't want that either. She wanted the fire and the sparks. She wanted a husband who looked like he'd been moonstruck just speaking her name, one whose promises she could rely on forever, who'd keep her safe and warm in the daylight hours, who'd make her skin tingle with excitement in the private nighttime hours. Thomas had kept her safe and warm, and she'd expected that the sparks would be there on their honeymoon.

It surprised her to realize that if they weren't there in the light of day, they wouldn't have been there when she'd donned her nightrail either. She thought about Adelida and the electricity between her and Rueben when he came in for dinner. The way that even after Ford was born Douglass' face lit up when Monroe touched her hand. Or the way Geneva's blue eyes danced when Reed was anywhere in sight. Not to mention the fire between Ellie and Colum. That's what Indigo wanted. Not a mere contented existence. She'd have it someday in the far, far future. Someday when she had hair again and when she could believe in promises.

"Beans," Adelida said, carting a whole bushel basket overflowing with long, skinny green beans to the porch. "Ellie said Thomas was here. Where did he go?"

"To deliver lumber, I suppose," Indigo said.

"And how are you?" Adelida raised a dark eyebrow.

"I'm fine. He just told me there was no fire, no spark between us. That's what he's got with Maudie he says. He'll die for her, so great is his love but all he expected with me was contentment."

"I'm glad, if it wasn't there between the two of you,

that you didn't marry him, Indigo. That's a marriage, but it's not love. And it's love that makes life worth living. I want you to have the spark and the fire," she said.

"Enough talk about fire and sparks. The only ones I see these days are when Flannon comes into my sight. That man can rile me quicker than anyone. Let's get at these beans. I'm surprised to see them still producing green this late in the year. I figured I'd be shelling them rather than snapping them. Will you get me an apron from the kitchen and a bowl? I can put the ends and strings in my lap that way."

Adelida smiled. Indigo would find her soulmate, and when she did she'd forgive Thomas. "Of course, I will. It's good to see you up and around. I told Ellie that you'd be out of that bed by tomorrow. One bullet or hurt foot can't keep a good woman down, and you are a strong lady."

"That I am," Indigo said.

Chapter Six

Indigo shivered as she watched the sun, barely a sliver of orange, dip below the mountains on the west side of Love's Valley. She'd stayed busy all day, keeping her mind off the inevitable hour when the doctor would arrive. Today was the day her bandages came off and she'd view herself as a bald woman. She'd been a tough, stubborn, self-willed, determined person her entire life, but the moment she heard his buggy wheels crunching through the yard and coming toward the bunk house, she wished she could curl up and whine.

"He's here." Flannon rapped lightly on her closed door.

"Send him on in," she called out, amazed that she could even speak through the fog of fear in her heart. She hobbled over to the mirror to stare at her reflection one more time with the bandages. Scary as they were, she would be sorry to lose them. At least they covered a bald head.

"Hello, Indigo." the doctor pushed his way into the room. "Come on in here, Flannon. I might need some help with something, and I see the women of the household have wisely kept themselves out of the way of Indigo's wicked tongue."

"Doc!" she exclaimed, turning as fast as she could without stumbling and falling at his feet.

"Never said I was a tactful person, now did I? Matter of fact, I'm about as tactless as you are," he teased, his dark eyes, buried in a pile of wrinkles, twinkled. He'd rather rile her and face a temper fit any day as try to comfort a weeping river of salty tears against his best suit.

"I couldn't hold a candle to you!" she huffed.

"He's crazy if he thinks he's as tactless as you are," Flannon muttered.

But Indigo heard it. "Don't you even start." She pointed her slim index finger at him, so close to his nose that it blurred when he stared down at it.

"No fighting like children or I'll send you both to a corner and make you rethink your ornery ways. Sit right here on this chair, Indigo, by the window and the light so I can see better. I don't think there's any infection or you would have had a fever by now. You are a lucky lady who owes Colum for that much. He's the one who discovered the manure pile where the bullet was dipped."

She sat still and someday she might thank Colum for his quick thinking, but today her insides were a quivering mess of nerves. She didn't want to even think about what she'd look like without hair. She hated thinking about staying in the valley a year or more until it grew back, but that's what she'd do. Be hanged to everyone who thought she was avoiding Thomas and Maudie. It would be hard enough to face her family with no hair and they all loved her—well, most of them . . . part of the time. Everyone except Flannon, and he could jump in the lake of fire right next to the devil's own playhouse if he thought for one minute she cared what he thought.

"Now, let's take a look." The doctor began unwinding the bandages. "Uh-huh, yes, uh-huh, looking very good. No infection here. Drain hole is even healing nicely. That's the only scab. Rest is sticking back together right well. Come on over here, Flannon, and take a look since you're the one who helped me get it all put back together. Looks right nice don't it?"

Flannon leaned forward, peering at the long line of stitches from one end to the other. Indigo was going to have a hissy fit when she looked in the mirror. The part that her hair wouldn't cover was a bit longer than he'd remembered, and for months it would have little holes where the needle pierced the skin. True enough—the gap at the back wasn't nearly as bad as it could have been. A scab about the size of a dime would be covered by her hair when it grew back in. What she was going to have a fit over was that nasty-looking stretch from her hairline across her forehead.

"Well, what do you think, son?" the old doctor asked.

"You did a fine job. Going to take those stitches out now?" Flannon asked.

"Yes, I am, then I'll wash it all up nice and Miss Indigo will be pretty as ever." He winked behind Indigo's back.

Flannon watched from a safe distance as the doctor removed twenty-one stitches, little black curly things that lay on top of the bandages like a family of freshly hatched baby spiders. Then he soaped up a washcloth and went about washing Indigo's head. It wasn't bald anymore. Not like it had been ten days before, all slick and shiny. Now it had a stubby covering, reminding Flannon of the time when he and his brothers got head lice and their grandmother shaved all their heads. Two weeks later their heads looked like the stubble in a wheat field after harvest. He didn't think Indigo would want to hear such a thing, so he kept his mouth shut.

"All done," the doctor said after he'd taken care of Indigo's head. "Now let's take a look at the ankle. Uh-huh, yep, coming along nicely," he muttered the whole time he pressed the bruises, now turning light green. "Be able to put a little weight on it in a couple of weeks, and then more as you feel you can. Not for two more weeks. It takes a sprain a long time to heal. You just obey me and maybe by the Hamilton harvest party, you'll be able to let this young man at least have a dance with you. Nothing spicy, like one of his Irish reels, but by the middle of October you might at least have a little slow dance."

"I don't think so. I wouldn't dance with him for the promise of a front seat in heaven," Indigo said indignantly. "Besides, who said we'd have a harvest party? We haven't had one since I was thirteen."

"War is over. Boys are all home. Besides I heard Reed mention it the other day when he brought that new baby of his in for me to take a look at," the doctor grinned.

"Is something wrong with Angelina?" Indigo asked, forgetting herself for a minute.

"No, nothing is wrong with her or Monroe's little boy, either, but Reed wanted me to take a look at her and make sure everything was all right. Since she hadn't had the benefit of a doctor at her birth and all, he was just being careful. Now, you be thinking about that harvest party and

I'll get on out of here. Got another house call to make before I get back to town." The doctor snapped his black bag shut and waved from the door.

"You go too," she told Flannon.

"Why wouldn't you dance with me, if I had a mind to ask you, that is?" he asked from the doorway.

"Because I don't dance with men I don't like and detest. Why waste time on someone you loathe?" she asked bluntly.

"Oh well, if that's the reason, I can live with it." He grinned. "For a minute there, I was afraid you didn't think I was handsome enough to be dancing with you."

She scowled and threw a pillow at him. It hit the shut door, and his laughter echoed through the whole bunk house. She sat still for ten minutes trying to muster the courage to get up and look in the mirror. Gingerly, she reached up and touched the bristles covering her head. In her mind's eye, she looked exactly like the owner of the hotel in Shirleysburg, a big, burly man who kept his thinning hair cut at about a quarter of an inch long.

A deep sigh filled the entire room. Instinctively, she reached for her crutches and set them just right under her arms. Shutting her eyes, she stood on her one good leg and turned ever so slowly toward the mirror hanging on the wall. She argued with herself for three minutes, saying it didn't matter what she looked like. She was at least alive and there had been no infection. That was something to be grateful for, now, wasn't it? Then she opened her eyes in a flash and saw the reflection of a hideous woman in the mirror staring back at her. Hot, steamy tears welled up, spilled from her dark blue eyes, running in streams down her cheeks and onto the front of her dress. The scar someday might be nothing more than a faint white line, but right then, even in the fading light of the day, it was an angry red line traveling from above her eye all the way back the side of her head. The holes where the stitches had been were red pin dots lined up against the scarlet line. Without blinking, she continued to gaze at the disfiguring injury. She'd almost gotten the tears under control when she saw the whole picture, not just the scar. Her glorious thick hair was gone. Nothing but stubble remained. She hadn't been wrong. Her hair did look like his, only where his was thinning and light, hers was thick and dark.

"Are you all right in there?" Flannon asked from the other side of the door. He'd expected wails of anguish at the very least: a storming rage, complete with broken windows and mirrors at the worst. He'd thought it would be wise to drape the mirror in her room with a tea towel to preserve his sanity and her vanity, but before he could do such a thing, the doctor had arrived.

"I. Am. Fine." She emphasized each word distinctly. She'd have to go to confession for sure for that blatant lie. She was anything but fine. She was disfigured and disgraced. Women didn't even cut their hair, not in polite social circles. They sure didn't shave their heads. She'd be confined to the farm for years waiting for enough hair to pull back into a proper chignon.

"Want me to get Geneva or Ellie?" He didn't believe for a minute that she was fine. If that had been Douglass, he and his brothers would have never heard the end of the carrying on. She would have locked herself in the cellar until it all grew back.

"I want you to go to bed and go to sleep and forget I'm in here. Don't you dare let anyone in this room," she declared.

Her tone left no doubt that he'd better do exactly what she said.

She took one long last look at the mirror.

I am strong. I can make it through this ordeal. If I can face off with Thomas and listen to him tell me he never loved me as much as he does Maudie, I can live without hair. If I can put up with that obstinate Rebel living right on the other side of the door, I can survive anything. After all, it's just a head of hair. It's not like I've been scalped and it will never grow back.

She didn't believe a word of it.

Flannon laced his fingers behind his head and wished desperately that he was home in Texas. It would be nearing harvest time there also, and the Sullivans and Montoyas always had the best fall festival in north Texas. It lasted at least three days, with dancing and parties every evening in the big barn. Horses were raced, traded, and bet on. Cattle was sold. Hay was bought and sold. There was enough food to feed an army with plenty to spare. And the women—ah, the women, arriving in their fancy dresses to flirt with the Sullivan men! At least what was left of them. Colum was married to Ellie, and Patrick would be spending every waking minute once he returned from the trip with his precious Maria. That would leave only Keven, Nick, and Brendon to do the Sullivan name proud.

He pictured Indigo at a Texas fall festival, with that long, flowing mane of dark hair iced with all those coppery highlights. With those deep, dark blue eyes and heavy lashes, she'd have the Texans falling at her feet—as long as she kept her mouth shut, that is. Lord Almighty, but that woman did have a sharp tongue. Ellie said it was just "her way," and Flannon respected Ellie's wisdom. But if that were the honest-to-goodness truth, then Indigo needed to change her way.

"It ain't happenin'," he whispered in a deep Texas drawl. "That woman will set every man's teeth on edge or cause him to bite his tongue right off before she changes. If she were the last woman on earth and there were only one man left, she'd scare him away with her words."

He shut his eyes and dreamed of a party in DeKalb, Texas. Indigo stepped out of a fancy carriage with a crest on the side. She wore a deep blue satin dress trimmed in white lace and sporting one of those little trains on the skirt that all the women seemed to like. She'd dressed her hair high in the Mexican fashion with a white lace mantilla flowing from the crown all the way down her back. She reached out her hand to him, and he led her to the dance floor where they danced the Irish reel perfectly, neither of them missing a single step in the wild, flamboyant dance. He held her tightly to his chest when the dance finished, and their hearts beat furiously in unison.

Then someone jerked the mantilla from her head and all her hair came with it. She gasped and ran away weeping loudly into the crowd. He tried to follow her, but the people closed in around him, keeping him back, pulling at his sleeves, telling him she was a Yankee. They yelled at him to forget the feeling he'd had when they danced. He ran but got nowhere. His heart pounded a mile a minute, but his feet were lead.

He awoke with a start, taking a few minutes to collect his bearings, to make the transition from what was dream to reality. He sat straight up in bed. A lonely cricket sang a haunting song in some far corner of the bunk house. A night owl added to the chorus, and Flannon strained his ears, expecting to hear a coyote put his lonesome voice into the mixture. For a brief moment, he thought he did hear a Texas coyote whining off somewhere in the far distance. Then he realized the cricket and owl were singing a duet. The whining and whimpering were coming from behind Indigo's door. He jerked his pants on over the top of his union suit and leaned his ear against the wood door.

"No, no. Please don't," she sobbed.

Flannon raced back across the long room in his bare feet, grabbed his Colt .45 from the holster hanging on his bed post and was inside her room, pointing the gun in every direction before the clock ticked off a full minute. He'd figured on finding a white-clad Klan member in the room, strangling Indigo or smothering her with a pillow, or maybe even worse. Not saying that he wouldn't be willing most days to strangle her himself. More than once a day she made him so mad he could eat railroad spikes and spit out ten penny nails. But he'd given his word that he would protect the woman, and protect her he would.

"No, please!" Indigo fought at the covers with her fists.

Flannon lowered the pistol and watched her. She was having a nightmare. For an instant, he wondered if it were possible to share a dream. Was she running from the people at the Texas fall festival? Was she begging them not to remove her hair?

Indigo dreamed of a whole band of renegade Rebels. They'd burned her home, and Love's Valley was full of smoke. Then they grabbed her by her long hair, and one of them had a knife to her scalp. He had paint smeared across his face and wore a buckskin loincloth, and the

Rebels called him Killer Wolf. They laughed when he tangled his fingers into her hair and flashed the knife in the moonlight. Suddenly, Flannon rode up on a big black horse. Killer Wolf said he'd scalp the Irishman even if he were a Southerner. No true Rebel would be rescuing a Yankee woman.

"Indigo, wake up." Flannon touched her arm.

She continued to sob and thrash about in the sheets.

He sat down on the edge of the bed and shook her arm gently. Moonlight streamed through the window, lighting up half her face and darkening the other half. Even with the scar showing so brightly in the moon rays, she was a beautiful woman.

"Indigo, it's just a dream. Wake up," he said loudly.

"Save me. Please save me. Don't let them." She sat straight up in bed, throwing her arms around Flannon's neck and burying her face in his chest.

"It's just a nightmare," he told her, wrapping his arms around her to keep her steady.

Indigo couldn't tell what was dream and reality. She just knew that suddenly the evil Indian and the Rebels faded into the gray fog and Flannon had dismounted from the big horse and was holding her tightly. Flannon had saved her scalp.

"They were going to kill me."

"It was just a nightmare."

"It was so real."

"I know. Dreams can be that way."

"But . . ." She pushed her face back away from his chest and looked at him. She was hugging Flannon Sullivan, in her bedroom, at night, with nothing between them but a thin cotton nightrail and his union suit. And the wildest thing was that it felt good.

"Indigo, I'm . . ." Words failed him. An Irishman, and suddenly the words had blown away on the night breezes. He traced a silvery line where tears had run down her cheeks and tilted her chin up with the edge of his thumb. He'd never noticed how full her mouth was, how much it begged to be kissed.

"Flannon?"

Then his mouth found hers.

Indigo was more prepared for the scalping in the nightmare than she was for the explosion that contorted her heart into a mass of trembling, quickening life. In the beginning it was sweet and gentle, and her stomach clenched into something akin to desire. Then it deepened, his tongue teasing hers into a mating dance that thrilled her soul. Sparks. Fire. Flames.

"I'm sorry." He pulled away and stood up so fast he knocked the chair beside her bed over with a loud bang. "I had no right to take advantage of your nightmare like that. I'll leave you now."

"I think you better. And don't you ever do that again. It was the dream, not me. I wouldn't want you to kiss me for anything. Don't you dare ever, ever tell that you did or I'll swear you are lying," she said. Not that she wanted him to go, but another one of those kisses and she'd be begging him to stay with her.

"It won't happen again."

"You are absolutely right," she declared. She wasn't stupid. She'd seen herself in the mirror. No man would be foolish enough to kiss a woman with no hair. Not even a half-Irish, half-Mexican Rebel. He'd never want anyone to know that he'd experienced a moment of weakness and kissed her the first time.

Was that what Thomas felt when he kissed Maudie?

She touched her lips to see if they were as hot as they felt. Could it be that was what happened every time people who were truly in love kissed? Not that she would ever fall in love with Flannon Sullivan. That wasn't even a possibility. She touched her mouth again and shivered deliciously as she remembered the effect his lips had on hers.

Sparks? They'd sure lit up her insides.

Fire? She was still flushed.

Flames? Another kiss, and the bunk house would be burning to the ground.

Well, now she knew. And that's what she'd look for when she went courting again. She'd never settle for anything less. Too bad it had to be Flannon who'd awakened her to the wisdom of sparks and fire in a relationship. But surely God wasn't so selfish as to put only one man on earth whose kisses could make her breathe like she'd run the whole length of Love's Valley.

She threw herself backward on the pillows and folded her hands over her bosom. Tomorrow she'd pretend it never happened because she had no intentions of ever letting that Yankee know how he'd affected her.

Flannon stretched out on his bed and shut his eyes. He'd kissed lots of girls, starting at fourteen with Maggie Desoto behind the barn at a fall festival. He'd even fancied himself in love last year and had entertained notions of asking Clara McLish to marry him. That had fallen through when she accepted the proposal of a horse trainer from Austin before Flannon got up the nerve to propose. But nothing had ever affected him like holding

Indigo Hamilton in his arms and feeling the heat between them.

Not Indigo! He wanted to shout into the valley. He could not let his silly heart fall in love with that woman. Not if he had to go through his whole life searching for a woman to set his soul on fire like she'd just done. Not if he was the only son in the Sullivan family to be a cantankerous old bachelor.

Chapter Seven

When dawn broke through the night and the sun lit up the valley, Indigo was standing in front of the mirror, trying in vain to get used to the woman staring back at her. If she couldn't face herself, then she couldn't expect the rest of the family to endure being in the same room with her.

"Indigo?" Geneva's soft Southern voice followed a light rap on the door.

"Come in." Indigo braced herself for the look of shock when Geneva saw her without her bandages.

"Look at you, all bandage free," Geneva said.

Indigo searched for pity or disgust in Geneva's face but found neither. "And hideous."

"Maybe so today. But in no time you'll be back to your old self again. Hair grows back. I'm just thankful you are alive. There's going to come a time when women are free to do what they want, Indigo. They'll vote, hold public office, and attend universities. And they'll even cut their hair and wear dresses that don't cover every square inch of their legs and arms. We might not live to see such a day, but it will come."

"What has that got to do with today?"

"Not a thing, except that we're going to pretend you're just a bit ahead of your time with your short hair even if you can't vote or be president. I brought a whole basket full of rags that I hemmed last night. I think there's one to match everything you have in your closet, including a lovely pale blue one covered in lace for Sundays. Mazell showed me how to make them."

"The slave woman you helped and got into trouble for? Why would you bring rags to me?" Indigo frowned.

"That's right, and I brought them so you wouldn't feel like a hideous spectacle when you leave this room. Sometimes if we cover up what scares us, it helps, or in your case it grows out. Mazell taught me how to wrap one of these things around my head when I was working to keep dust and grime out of my hair. I figure it will also cover up your head until your hair is a little longer," Geneva said.

"I'm not scared, and don't you dare call me a hideous spectacle."

"I didn't. I said you feel like one. You just said that yourself, so don't get on a high horse with me. I'm trying to help."

"Okay, I'd try anything right now." Indigo's interest was piqued.

"Now sit down right here. First we wrap this part around your forehead. Don't quite cover the whole scar, and then this side goes down the back, and this part tucks up, and there we go, all fixed. Take a look in the mirror."

"Oh, my, it's wonderful," Indigo turned this way and

that. True a bit of her scar did show but still, she didn't look like a freak. "Can you show me how to do it?"

"Sure. I brought a bunch so you can use a fresh one every day of the week, and this pretty lacy one is for Sunday."

"I'm not going to church. I'm not leaving the valley until I'm human again." Indigo touched the turbanlike scarf on her head and actually smiled.

"Flannon said you'd be able to go this week."

"Flannon Sullivan isn't God. He doesn't make decisions for me. He's . . ." Ice hung on her words, even the ones she couldn't get out of her mouth. She blushed, remembering the kiss from the night before.

Geneva laughed. Not a girly giggle she hid behind her hand, but a big, full-fledged roar, where she threw her head back and lost her breath. "So he's got you riled up again, does he? Men can sure do that in a hurry, and just when we think we don't ever want to see another one. After Hiriam was hanged, I didn't want to get involved with another worthless man, and before he was even in his grave, there was your brother sitting across from me in the stagecoach, looking down his nose on me for being dirty and fat."

"I still can't believe you married him after that, but just because my brother was there and you fell in love with him does not mean that I'm about to fall in love with Flannon Sullivan. I'm not stupid; I can see what you are doing, telling me how much you fought with your husband. Well, it's different with Flannon. I absolutely despise him and always have. If he were the only prospect of marriage, I'm afraid I'd be an old maid. Let's not talk about him. Just his name sets me into a mad spell. Now that I'm all fixed up for the day, help me climb the back stairs to the kitchen. I can sit at the table and at least help get dinner done for the hired help."

Flannon arose early. He skipped breakfast, grabbing a hunk of bread and a piece of cheese on his way through the dark kitchen of the main house in search of a cup of cold coffee before he went out to the work site. The walls were up on Ellie and Colum's new home. The roof was finished. Today he was going to set in the windows and glaze in the glass. It was a tedious job and slow going, but he could do it alone.

He strapped on his leather work belt and was well into having the first six-pane window done by the time Colum arrived. Flannon could hardly believe his eyes when he had read Colum's letter last spring saying he was staying in Love's Valley and he'd married Ellie. The very woman who'd scratched and scarred him for life, and here he was, happily married, whistling at daybreak because he was building a home right in the middle of Yankee territory. The war was over, but who'd have believed such a story about Douglass or Colum two years ago?

" 'Bout time you came to work," Flannon mumbled around a mouthful of small nails.

"Spit out those nails. You know what Grandfather told you about holding them in your mouth while you work. One of these days you're going to swallow a whole mouth full and die of a ruptured gut," Colum told him.

"Mmm-huh," Flannon grunted and kept working.

"And what brought on that mean Irish scowl, Flannon Romano Sullivan?" Colum asked. "Why'd you miss break-fast? In all my life, I've never seen you without an appetite."

"None of your business," Flannon spit out the final nail and tapped it into place to hold the glass pane while he glazed it.

"Indigo giving you fits out there in that bunk house? I don't envy you that job one bit. You'll be ready to light a shuck to Texas at the first sign of spring and I won't blame you a bit, even if we will miss you. Most likely you'll marry the first little filly who winks at you just to get the memory of that sharp-tongued woman out of your mind," Colum teased.

"Why don't you go to work? Winter is coming. You and Ellie would like to be in your own place, wouldn't you?"

"Whew, only one thing can make a Sullivan use a tone like that. Got to be a Hamilton woman or man. I remember when me and Ellie was snowed in up in that cabin and when we had to walk down out of Blacklog Valley. She could rile me up just with a look. What has Indigo done now?" Colum picked up his own work belt and strapped it around his hips.

"Nothing. Not one thing," Flannon declared. "I just want to get this job done so I can start on Rueben's place. Would be nice if you didn't want to jaw around all day instead of working is all."

"She's gotten under your skin, little brother." Colum grinned. "The whole bunch of them are an impossible lot until you tame them. Then they make right good partners. It's just the taming that's hard work."

"Indigo wouldn't make a partner for anyone. She's spoiled and the most hateful woman on the face of the earth. If all you're going to do is talk, then I'm stopping work too."

Colum whistled as he walked away without a word,

which infuriated Flannon even more than if he'd slugged him in the face.

Flannon figured if he had a lick of sense, he'd be saddling up his horse and riding out of Love's Valley before dinnertime. He'd said he'd stay, but he could make some kind of excuse and get out before winter set in. Or he could just wait until night and ride out without even a good-bye. His brother and sister would understand. Neither one of them offered to babysit Indigo, the ultimate shrew. Maybe by spring he truly would be married to the first filly who winked at him. He'd at least give it his best effort.

"Hey, you missed breakfast. Are you ailing?" Ellie asked right behind him.

"No, just wanted to get an early start," Flannon said.

"I want this house as soon as we can get it done, but I don't want you to work yourself to death." She patted him on the shoulder. "Hey, you should see what Geneva made for Indigo. These head rag things that some ex-slave taught her how to use. They're just squares of cloth, but Geneva knows how to wrap them just so and they sure made Indigo feel better."

"I'm surprised that she accepted them from a Southerner," Flannon groused.

"So were the rest of us. Adelida told Geneva she was wasting her time making them last night. Guess vanity won out over pride. Seen Colum?"

"Upstairs," Flannon said. Why was everyone in such a good mood today? He wanted to whip a rabid coyote barehanded or kick the devil from a drunk in a barroom brawl, and the rest of the family wanted to talk about Indigo. She didn't need a rag on her head to look good to him. She was beautiful even with a scar and no hair. She made his heart do double time when she hugged him. Flames shot through his ears when they kissed.

"Grouch," Colum said right behind him as he reloaded his belt with nails. "Guess it comes with the territory."

"And this grouch could leave the territory anytime," Flannon smarted back.

"But he won't." Colum slapped him on the shoulder and went back to work.

It was as if the whole family knew exactly what had happened the night before. Darnit! Indigo had to have gone out first thing this morning and told the women about the kiss. His cheeks burned with a crimson blush.

At noon he washed up with the rest of the hired hands at the pump beside the back porch, dried his hands on the towels hanging on a nail, and sat down at the long table set up under the shade trees. Adelida, Ellie, Douglass, and Geneva carted bowls and platters laden with ham, fried chicken, mashed potatoes, yams, green beans, hot yeasty rolls, corn on the cob, and gravy. Thirty men set about eating.

Flannon loaded his plate. The meager breakfast had long since failed him, and he was truly hungry. He listened to the fellow next to him talk about his new wife and how they'd found a house to buy. Nothing, it seemed, would suit him better than getting his wife out of the house away from his mother. There wasn't a house big enough in the world for two women, according to him.

Yet, there had been lots more than two women living in the Hamilton house. They appeared to get along most of the time, anyway. At least until Indigo let her mouth get ahead of her good sense and one of them had to set her straight. However, that didn't happen often, hardly at all since he'd moved Indigo out to the bunkhouse.

He scanned the area, looking for Indigo. He didn't really wanted to see her, just wondered where she might be was all.

"Dessert arrives." Geneva set a chocolate cake on each end of the table. "I'm not rushing you fellers. Just getting it out here for the fast eaters. Adelida is bringing out apple pies too."

"Good food, Miz Hamilton," one of the hands commented.

"Always is. One thing about working in Love's Valley is that they pay on time and feed you well," an old-timer said between bites.

"Thank you," Reed said. "We've got some good cooks."

Indigo opened the back door and eased out. The rag on her head did cover up the fact she had no hair, Flannon noticed. It was the same color blue as her eyes and if she'd had gold hoops in her ears, she could have passed for one of the beautiful gypsy girls in the band that came in the spring to help with the horses in Texas. She avoided his eyes when he looked up, and that convinced him even more that she'd been inside the house telling everyone about the kiss. Tonight they'd all tell their husbands, and tomorrow there would be three Hamilton brothers out for blood. No doubt about it, tonight would be the last night they trusted him to protect their little sister from the Klan.

She went into the bunk house and quietly shut the screen door. She couldn't be around all the newlyweds another minute or she was going to explode. She was sick nigh unto death with watching all that love. She'd partaken of the fountain of knowledge with that miraculous kiss the night before. Now she knew what it was they shared and what she didn't have.

"I've got to get my knife." Flannon mumbled an excuse for leaving the table before he had dessert. "Be back in a minute." There was no way he could work all afternoon and into the dusk of evening without knowing. One thing for sure was that Indigo would tell him the truth.

"Indigo?" He rapped gently on her bedroom door.

"Come in."

"I wanted to . . ." He stared at her. Her steely blue eyes looked huge with nothing but a rag on her head.

"You wanted to tell me you were sorry for kissing me again. Don't worry, Flannon, I'm as ashamed of myself for letting you kiss me as you are for doing it. It will never happen again. And please don't go brandishing it about among the men folk out there. They'd take it the wrong way and say that I'm just latching on to you to have a husband since Thomas dumped me at the altar and I'm bald. They'll say that I think anything is better than nothing. Even a half-Irish, half-Mexican Rebel. I don't want their pity or your kisses."

"Then you didn't tell the womenfolk?"

"Good Lord, no! I'm not telling anyone. I'd have to admit you were in my bedroom and sitting on my bed. No, Flannon, I won't tell a soul and neither will you. Promise me that." If anyone could scream in a whisper, Indigo was doing it.

"You got it," he said tersely. Half Irish. Half Mexican. All Rebel. They all disgusted the prim and proper Miss Indigo Hamilton.

Well, good luck, honey, on ever finding anyone who can make you swoon like I did.

"I don't like you. Matter of fact, I think you're a rogue for taking advantage of my nightmare like that. I can't stand you," Indigo said hatefully.

"Likewise," he snapped.

"So are we back to normal?"

"Better than normal. We're all the way back to the first time we met." He stormed out the door.

"That's wonderful," she said. "Just wonderful."

Her lips said the words.

Her soul knew she was lying.

Her heart wept.

Chapter Eight

"I'm not surprised, but I'd hoped you would go with us this morning," Geneva told Indigo.

"Oh?" Indigo fussed with a head rag getting it just right before she left her bedroom. The doctor had returned a couple of weeks before and announced that her foot was progressing well enough that she could begin putting weight on it. The first time she tried, she almost tumbled to the floor, but since then she'd grown stronger.

"Yes, Adelida and Douglass have a bet going with Flannon. They say you're tough enough to tame a bayou 'gator or a Texas cougar, and you'll go to church today. Flannon says you might do either of those but you won't go to church on the day we stay and clean the cemetery because you'd have to face Thomas and Maudie for more than an hour and you're only ninety percent tough. The other ten percent is bluff and he thinks you are bluffing right now."

Indigo's eyes narrowed into mere slits. "What's the bet?"

"Five dollars," Geneva said.

"Flannon would lose ten dollars if I go. Adelida and Douglass each lose five if I don't," she pondered, already taking off the head rag and reaching for the fancy lace one reserved for Sunday and never worn.

"Does that mean you are going or that you're just dressing up to spend the whole day alone?"

"Oh, honey, I'm going all right," Indigo said, amazed that she'd picked up on the Southern slang. She'd been so careful up to now to keep all the *honey*s and *darlin*'s out of her speech, and there it was right out of her mouth, and by all that was sacred, if it didn't even have a Southern lilt to it! She'd have to be very careful with all these Southern women around her all day. "I'd go bare naked and without anything to cover my head in order to see Flannon have to dish out ten dollars."

"Then which dress shall I get out of the wardrobe for you to wear?"

"I'll go get it." Indigo tied the knot at the nape of her neck and tucked the ends of the lace square down just right without looking in the mirror. Since the day Geneva brought her the head rags, she'd learned to cover her head without the benefit of the mirror. The idea of looking at herself again and having those nightmares was enough to bring on the vapors plus a case of hives, so she avoided the mirror and shut her eyes when she got anywhere near it. "I can get up the stairs with one crutch and what weight I can put on my foot. I may even stay in my own room from now on."

"If you really think you're ready, I'm sure Flannon will be more than glad to have you out of his way," Geneva said.

"Has he been talking?" Indigo's eyes flashed.

"No, nothing like that. Matter of fact, if I didn't know better, I'd say he's quite smitten with you. Got to be an old bear these past few weeks. Ever since that day when he left the table and said he had to come to the bunk house and get his knife. Now, I'm not a betting woman, but I'd be thinking that the two of you had words that day. Want to tell me what they were about?"

"No, I do not," Indigo said.

So they *had* had a fight of some sort, Geneva thought as she walked across the yard, fall leaves crunching beneath her feet. She and Ellie, along with Adelida and Douglass, had figured the only thing that would make them both so cross and miserable had to be a big argument. The four of them had even remembered aloud the days when the Hamilton and Sullivan men had affected them the exact same way. Geneva wondered what it was about and if Flannon was the person to tame Indigo. It would take nothing short of a miracle from heaven to make that girl wake up and smell the beauty of love.

"Oh, is the pampered and spoiled princess going to church?" Flannon looked up from the dining room table where he lingered over another cup of coffee.

"I'm not pampered and I'm not nearly as spoiled as one lousy old Rebel named Flannon Sullivan. And yes, I'm going to Mass and then I'm staying for the picnic. Wouldn't miss the fall cemetery cleaning and visiting with all my friends for anything, so you can cough up ten dollars," she said.

"I see the sisters have been talking." Flannon hated losing a bet, but this time it would be worth it.

"Yes, but I'd already made up my mind to go anyway, so you lost money you didn't have to lose," she lied.

"The luck of the Irish fails me today." He rolled his eyes as he left to help get the two buggies ready for the trip. Of course she wasn't telling the truth and had no thought of spending the day outside Love's Valley before Geneva so slyly let the cat out of the bag about the bet. He had to admire Indigo's spunk, though. Beautiful, spunky, and like Adelida said, tough as a bayou 'gator. Someday when she awoke to her own worth, she'd do for any man to hitch up with for the ride down the river of life. Any man but Flannon Sullivan who wasn't spending but one winter in Love's Valley—to get Colum into his own house, then to help get Rueben and Adelida's started. Reed and Geneva would have to depend on the rest of the family to build their home, because he'd be long gone to Texas before that foundation was laid.

The front door opened in a few minutes and Hamiltons and Sullivans paraded out in their Sunday finery. Douglass and Monroe with little Ford all wrapped up in blue blankets crawled into the first buggy, followed by Reed and Geneva and a pink bundle. Rueben helped Adelida up into the driver's seat to sit beside him and then picked up the reins, flicked the horses on their flanks, and started up the lane. Colum opened the door of the second buggy for Ellie and then helped Indigo inside. Flannon saw to it that they were comfortable before he settled into the driver's seat and followed closely behind the first buggy.

The aroma of fried chicken hiding in the food baskets inside the second coach wafted through the fresh morning breezes and tickled Flannon's nose. He'd never been to a cemetery picnic and thought it more than a little bit morose when the Hamiltons first mentioned it. After Mass, the whole church stayed for a picnic on the grounds, and each member took care of their ancestors' graves, pulling weeds, making sure the tombstones were standing straight, and general upkeep. The whole afternoon was spent on quilts under the trees, eating and visiting after the cemetery duties.

"It's like a social," Reed had told him. "We take care of the gravesites all year, so there's little to do but visit them and remember the family buried there. Mostly, the women folk corral the children and trade gossip while the men gather to discuss politics. We haven't had a social like this since before the war, so everyone at the church is looking forward to it."

Flannon didn't look forward to politicking with the Yanks one bit. He was grateful that Colum would at least be there to back him up in case of a fight. He did look forward to biting into a good healthy chicken leg, though, and the sooner the better. He hoped Mass wouldn't last too long and dinner would be served early.

Indigo wondered what she was doing in the buggy. She hadn't been inside the church since the day of her wedding more than a month before, hadn't seen anyone outside of the family and the hired hands since that day either. Her stomach threatened to heave up her breakfast. Her hands grew clammy inside her soft leather gloves. Her head itched beneath the lace scarf tied perfectly around her head. The satin bow under her chin, holding on a fall hat she'd meant to wear on her honeymoon, choked her almost into a case of the vapors.

"I'm glad you're going with us today." Ellie patted Indigo's arm.

"Yes, ma'am, I am too," Colum said, his Texas drawl as deep as it was the first day he came to Love's Valley.

"You're not a hermit, Indigo. 'Tis time for you to get out and see people again."

"Are you ever going to talk like one of us?" Indigo snapped.

"Not if I have my way." Ellie touched his face lovingly.

Indigo turned to look at the familiar countryside. Anything to avoid the sparks between Colum and Ellie.

"Then I guess that answers it. If the wife likes this old Texas brogue, then I will certainly keep it, darlin'." He leaned forward and brushed a brief kiss across Ellie's soft lips.

Indigo didn't see it, but she heard it. She remembered the kiss she'd shared with Flannon and wondered if Ellie's insides were melting into a pool of something akin to soft butter. She turned just enough to see the soft blush turning Ellie's cheeks a rosy pink, and guessed they probably were.

She went back to staring out the window. She'd think about what the day might bring, whether she'd see any of her old friends, anything at all but the warmth of Colum and Ellie's love heating up the inside of the coach. Mother Nature was busy these days putting on quite a show. Maple trees were sporting brilliant burgundy, vibrant yellow, and bright orange leaves. Chicory, some of it head high, contributed its tiny blue flowers to the palette. When they got into town and turned toward the church located between Shirleysburg and Orbisonia, Indigo noticed flower boxes on porches and in yards filled with mums, carnations, and the last of the summer roses still trying to outdo their fall sisters. Nature's attempt to make her stop thinking about the intensity of her feelings failed miserably, and by the time they reached the church she'd stopped enjoying the lovely fall morning. All she could think about was Flannon Sullivan sitting up there on his perch and the way his kiss made her knees weak.

I hate him. I do. Why did he kiss me? Why, God, did you let him be the one who made me see what it's like to really kiss a man? It's not fair. First the failed wedding. My head shaved. Now a rotten Rebel everywhere I look. Listen to me, God! I've had enough. Send him away. Make my hair grow faster. I don't want patience. I want results.

Flannon parked on the west side of the church and Colum helped the two women from the coach. Flannon jumped down from the driver's seat and handed Indigo her crutches. By the time she got them positioned and fluffed out her skirt, everyone else was already entering the church. All but Flannon, who waited patiently to escort her inside.

She couldn't very well refuse to go through the doors with him without creating a scene. All the hired hands knew she lived in the bunk house with Flannon. They knew he was her bodyguard, so maybe everyone wouldn't think anything of the two of them arriving together.

He held the door open for her and followed her all the way up the center aisle to the Hamilton pews at the front of the church where two spaces had been left for them. Indigo sat ramrod straight, hoping that her tense muscles would fight off the emotional upheaval that arose when Flannon sat down, his shoulder touching hers. It didn't work.

Maybe if she looked at him. Really gave him a hard stare and reminded herself that he was a Rebel she'd get her old feelings of revulsion back. It was his kind who had burned Ellie's house, taken her father and mother from her. His kind who'd sent so many of Shirleysburg's finest young men to their graves or back home, maimed for life. It was his kind who'd caused the war to begin with, and if Thomas hadn't been out fighting for what was right, he would have never met Maudie. So her whole sorry tale of woe was Flannon's fault. She cut her eyes around to give him a drop-dead-and-stay-there look, only to find him staring right back at her. Even though it was childish, she snarled her nose and moved away from his touch.

Flannon winked, knowing that would infuriate her more than anything. Even through layers and layers of skirt and who knew how many petticoats to keep that dress swishing and poofed out, his thigh warmed at her touch. Her shoulder against his brought about a deep desire to throw his arm around her right there in church. But a gentleman didn't do that. Men didn't put their arms around their women in church. Not even if they were wives. That could be terms for instant excommunication. According to Grandmother Montoya, some things were all right in the parlor among married people, but the church was no place for displays of affection. It was where you went to get right with God, not right with your wife or husband. Heaven help any young man who attempted to flirt in the church. The Pope wouldn't have been any stricter than Grandmother Montoya.

Too bad it wasn't her arm that was sprained or even broken, and then he'd have an excuse to hold the hymnal for her, maybe brushing her fingertips with his. Colum was allowed to do that. Share the prayer book and hymnal with his wife, but they were married. The Father slowly walking down the aisle brought Flannon back to reality, jerking his mind and heart out of dreamland at the same time. By all that was holy, what had he been thinking about? This was Indigo Hamilton. He'd never actually hated anyone in his whole life, but he'd hated that female from the first time he met her. Now, here he was entertaining notions of putting his arm around her and drawing her close. He must have a fatal fever to even consider such a thing. He'd find someone at this picnic to flirt with even if it was the homeliest girl this side of Texas. He'd been too long without a woman in his life if Indigo was looking good.

He tried to pay attention to the services, bowing his head to pray at the right times, singing when he was supposed to, but visions of Indigo kept getting in his way. The memory of how she felt in his arms and the warmth of her lips heated up every fiber in his whole body.

Indigo kept her eyes away from Flannon. She didn't need to look at him to envision that slight dimple on the left side of his cheek. To see his brown eyes light up in mischief when he was teasing. To feel his presence so close even if it might as well have been six miles away back in Love's Valley, because she wasn't about to admit any kind of emotional feelings for the man. Not even if he was so handsome he took her breath away, or if his lips on hers made her want to spend her whole life kissing him.

God, we had a conversation before I came in here. Why haven't you done anything? By the time I leave this church I expect you to take care of this. I didn't come here for nothing today, you know.

"Indigo?" Thomas Brewster's voice broke into her heavenly demands. Everyone was already filing outside and Flannon held her crutches out to her, a mocking smile on his face. She wanted to slap it off, leaving a red handprint behind to remind herself that she wasn't affected one bit by him.

She braced herself on the pew in front of her and stood up as gracefully as possible, took the crutches from Flannon, and raised an eyebrow at Thomas.

"I would like to introduce you properly to my wife, Maudie, and our son, Tommy Junior. We call him T. J."

"Hello," Indigo said to the small, red-haired woman beside Thomas. Maudie wore a light blue dress trimmed in navy. Her thick hair was piled high on her head, and even the freckles scattered across her face were cute. A pang of pure jealousy for all that hair and the petite size shot through Indigo like a bolt of white lightning, leaving behind a bitter taste in her mouth.

"Miss Hamilton." Maudie held her gloved hand out.

"Mrs. Brewster." Indigo propped herself on one crutch and shook hands with the woman who'd upset her whole life.

"We'd best be getting on. I'll need to help unload lunch and quilts." Flannon tucked Indigo's elbow into his hand. There was enough tension in the air that Flannon would have bet his fancy boots a cat fight was in the making. Indigo had used up the limit of her niceties and could very easily commence to yanking Maudie's red hair out by the handful any moment. If he hadn't just lost ten dollars on a bet about Indigo, he would have put his money on the woman as mean as a bayou 'gator if push came to shove.

"Yes, I expect we'd better. It was nice meeting you properly," Indigo said coldly.

"And you," Maudie slipped her arm through Thomas' and looked up adoringly into his face. "We'd better get T. J. outside and find a spot for our quilt, darlin'. The poor baby's stomach was growling during Mass." The look she shot over her shoulder toward Indigo would have caused snow in hell.

"That witch," she muttered as Flannon led her down the aisle. "I could scratch every freckle off her nose."

"My grandmother always said you could catch more flies with honey than vinegar. You need to learn to be sweet even if it's against your nature."

"Don't you tell me how to act with a Southern witch. I hate her almost as much as—" she stopped abruptly.

"As me?" Flannon finished.

"That's what I started to say, but that's not possible," Indigo snapped.

"Oh, and I was just about to fall in love with you," he said sarcastically.

"I'm not a fly so don't try a honey approach with me. I know you feel the same way I do. I may throw a party when you go back to Texas."

"I may send a message and tell Momma to have one ready when I get home. With all the sweet, young, pretty women in the whole county invited."

"I hope the ugliest one catches you and you stay in Texas forever."

"I wouldn't care what she looked like long as she doesn't have your smart mouth. Darlin', you can bet your last dollar on the fact I'll stay there forever. If I ever get out of here, I'm never coming back."

"That's the best news I've head all day. There is a God in heaven."

A brisk fall breeze picked up as soon as Flannon opened the door for Indigo. The churchyard was already dotted with multicolored quilts, and he could see the

Hamilton and Sullivans claiming the rights to a shade tree not far from their buggies. Indigo made it slowly down the steps to the yard, and the wind tipped her hat forward over her eyes. Flannon was busy figuring out the best way to go from the church across the yard to the family dinner and wasn't paying a bit of attention to her. Until he heard her gasp and turned, ready to catch her if she'd gotten off balance.

The hat was gone, blowing across the grass toward the road. The next thing the wind claimed was the head rag, sending it floating across the air like a puffy, white cloud. It came to rest in a fresh pile of horse manure, right beside the hat, which had landed in a mud puddle.

"Get it! Don't just stand there!" she shouted.

Everyone turned to see what the to-do was all about.

She wanted to curl up in a ball and disappear. There she stood, jilted, scarred, bald, forsaken, and pitied. Not five feet from the beautiful Maudie Brewster.

"Well, look at you." Flannon stared at her as if she were some kind of queen decked out in royal apparel complete with a gold, diamond-encrusted crown.

"I would rather not," she whispered, mortified.

"I expect that head rag and your hat are both ruined, seeing where they landed," he said.

"Take me home, right now. I can't stay here." She felt her cheeks burning with embarrassment.

"Why not? You are lovely, Miss Indigo Hamilton. Take my arm and pretend you are the most beautiful woman here. Right now. Give me one crutch and use the other one for balance and let me lead you to the quilt. Don't give in to fear. They'll make a big deal out of it if you do. Pretend you don't give a damn."

Without thinking, she did exactly what he did, hoping that even a small part of her dignity could be saved with the gesture. Flannon was right. To run away would just give the people more to gossip about, more to cluck their tongues over, more to pity her for. She'd hold her head upright and later when she was home and in her own room, then she'd fall apart and cry until her eyes were swollen. She was entitled. She'd fought tears for a month. Four weeks of pure old torture and she fully well intended to have a screaming fit when she got home.

There she was right out in public. She'd never be the beauty that Maudie Brewster was anyway, and now she was hairless, with swollen eyes and an embarrassed, blotched face. She was fully well entitled to cry until tomorrow morning when she got home.

"Oh, my." Geneva looked up from the quilt. "What happened to your hat?"

"The wind got it and it landed in a mud hole. My head rag is over there covering up a fresh pile of horse manure. I don't plan on retrieving them. The smell would never come out of the lace, and the hat decorations are ruined," Indigo said.

"Well, you don't need either one," Adelida said from the center of the quilt where she was unloading several baskets of food. "I can't believe how fast your hair has grown. I wonder if it will ever be acceptable for women to cut all their hair off and look like you do. Wouldn't it be a blessing not to have to fix hair every morning?"

"What?" Indigo asked cautiously. Surely they were all just trying to make her feel less conspicuous. She glanced around at the rest of the people, putting out food on their quilts. They'd looked at her when she yelled at Flannon to get her hat, but now they were busy taking care of their own business. No one was staring at her like she had three eyes and horns sprouting out of her head.

"Your hair has grown back," Flannon told her bluntly. "You aren't bald. Didn't you notice when you washed it?"

"Not really. I haven't looked in the mirror in weeks," she said.

"Well, it's not bristles anymore," he said. "Feel it, Indigo. It reminds me of a little slave girl's hair. All kinky curly. Only yours is dark brown, where a slave child's would be black as coal."

She reached up and ran her fingers through tight curls that lay close to her head. They couldn't be more than an inch and a half long, but she really wasn't bald and the bristles were gone. She didn't look like a man. Among the socialites she'd be a rebel of the worst kind until it grew back, but she wasn't a disgrace. A rebel! She practically choked on the word.

"See, it's nice. No more bald. I never knew your hair was so curly." Ellie fluffed a few curls down on Indigo's forehead.

"It's always had lots of body and the ends were curly."

You did hear me, didn't you, God? Thank you for this much. Now could you get to work on the rest of it?

"Well, it's cute," Douglass said. "You sure don't need to cover it up anymore."

"Hey, look at our sister." A wide grin split Reed's face as he carried another basket to the site. "She looks like she did the day she was born. Remember that cap of black curls all over her head and those big old blue eyes. That's why Daddy named her Indigo. Said her eyes gave him the idea."

Indigo's spirits lifted up from the dirt to the heavens. "Then I wish my eyes would have been brown. I have hated this name."

"You hate everything and everyone who don't cater to your every whim. You mean you aren't going to name your first daughter Indigo?" Flannon said.

"It's none of your business, Mr. Irish Rebel, what I name my children. But no, I'll name her Sally or Liz or Sue. Anything but Indigo."

"It's not as bad as Herman Monroe," Douglass laughed, remembering the day she learned that Monroe's first name was Herman and the fit of giggles it brought about. "Herman was an old drunk in DeKalb that all of us kids were afraid of. He smelled horrible. You can't imagine how funny it was when I found out Monroe's name was Herman."

"That's respectable compared to my name," Indigo said.

"Oh, I don't know. I thought maybe we'd name our first daughter Indigo, after her auntie," Adelida said.

"You do and she'll grow up and never speak to you." Indigo was suddenly caught up in the light mood.

"Dinner is ready," Ellie announced. "Colum, you can offer grace and we'll eat. Then you men folks can go talk wars and rumors of wars while we women take care of the important matters of the world."

Colum raised a dark eyebrow. "And that would be?"

"It's a secret. That's what this day is all about. We set things straight and then go home and make you men folks think it was all your idea. Last time we had one of these, though, we had a bit of trouble with your hard-headedness and you went to war when we didn't want you to do so," she slipped her arm through his.

Colum bowed his head without an argument and said grace. He'd learned that sometimes it was wise to let Ellie think she was right.

Indigo felt Flannon's presence so close to her side she could have touched his hand while everyone had their heads bowed, but she didn't. He hadn't made any bones about the fact that he disliked her and was only serving as her protector because there was no one else to do the job.

God, you made my hair come back. Now make him go away. I can't take this turmoil any longer. I will not fall for a Rebel. I refuse. So send him home before the winter sets in or else strike him dead. I don't care which.

Flannon wished he and Indigo might have met on different terms, like down in Texas at a barn dance. Miracles had happened with Colum and Ellie, with Douglass and Monroe. And he suspected they'd happened in the case of Rueben and Adelida as well as Reed and Geneva. However, it would take something more akin to magic to make Indigo ever look at him and see a hardworking man instead of an Irish-Mexican Rebel, all three of which she couldn't abide. As Irish as he was, Flannon didn't believe there was that much magic in the whole world.

Chapter Nine

Indigo opened the wrought-iron gate to the fenced enclosure where the Hamiltons were buried: great-great-grandparents, grandparents, children who never made it to adulthood, her father. Even with the disappointments of having all three of her brothers bring home Southern wives, she was still glad they were alive, and she wasn't looking at their tombstones that Sunday afternoon. She sat down on the iron bench beside the gate and thought about her father, Harrison Hamilton. He'd been a big man, more than six feet tall, but gentle and kind, and she had no doubt that he absolutely adored her when he was alive.

Daddy, I've made a pickle of a mess out of my life. I really thought Thomas was the right man for me to marry, and at the last minute Maudie showed up. Now I've got strange feelings for this Rebel who's an Irishman and a Rebel to boot. I know his brother and Ellie get along fine so there would be a possible hope for him, but I really do despise him. How can a woman have two opposing emotions in her heart? I'm going to fight this, Daddy. I won't admit anything other than disgust for his kind. I can just avoid him. They say if you don't feed something, it will starve. So I'll stay out of his path and not think about him at all. Isn't that what I should do, Daddy? I've told God to strike him dead if all else fails.

"Nice little plot," Flannon said so close she could feel the warmth of his breath on her neck. Shivers trailed up and down her spine.

"What are you doing here?"

"Came to see where your father is put to rest. Tell you one thing, Indigo, I'm sure glad my own father hasn't passed. He takes care of everything," Flannon said.

"Oh, and what does everything entail?"

"About a hundred and fifty square miles of property. Horses, cattle, hay, all that goes into a ranch in Texas. And the Sullivan property in Ireland. Uncle Brendon does most of that. He comes to America every other year to discuss the business. He says he's getting old and one of us is going to have to go to Ireland. Probably his namesake, Brendon, who wants to go so bad he can taste it." Flannon leaned on the fence only a few feet from her, close enough he could see each individual curl on her head.

Holy Mary, Mother of Christ, she hadn't asked for a story, just a simple question to cover her own embarrassment—anything to keep him talking while she regained her composure. After all, one minute she'd been communing with her dead father, the next she was all tingly inside.

"I see," she said, the realization of what he'd said soaking in. The property he lived on was thirty times bigger than Love's Valley. That didn't even take into consideration the Irish part of the family's real estate.

"So would you ever want to go to Ireland?" he asked.

"Sure, I'd love to have a trip outside of Huntingdon County. But I wouldn't go anywhere with you, so if you're asking to take me, the answer is no," she said sharply.

"Girl, I'd take a mongrel before I'd ask you, so don't get your dander up. You've never traveled? I'd have figured you and your brothers, as wealthy as you all are, would have been everywhere." He opened the gate and sat next to her on the bench, careful to keep a healthy foot of air between them. Eyes would be watching. Tongues would be wagging. No need making things worse for Indigo. After all, she had to stay in Huntingdon County. He'd go home to Texas next spring.

"We might have, but the world fell apart. Daddy died and there was a year of mourning. Then the war came, and you know the rest. The money to travel wasn't the issue. All my brothers were off fighting. Momma and Ellie and I held down Love's Valley. Now it's too late," she said.

"It's never too late. Never say never, Indigo. It limits the possibilities."

"How would you know?"

"I just know. I suppose we'd best get on back to the rest of the family."

"Why?" She didn't budge.

"Because I can act as your bodyguard and help you back down the hill to the family, but if I stay too long, there'll be gossip. Actually, I didn't have anything else to do. Men are gathered in pockets remembering this battle or that one. I'd fit in about as well as a cow chip in a punch bowl at a fancy wedding. Colum and Ellie have taken a walk. Adelida, Geneva, and Douglass are playing house with real babies."

"So I'm just a diversion to keep you out of jail." She still didn't move.

"Out of jail?"

"Sure. If you join the men folks talking about the Yankee victories, that Mexican temper of yours will override any good sense you might have gotten from your Irish father, and you'll wind up in a fight. So I'm just a means to keep you occupied and out of trouble."

"I'm not so sure I'd put it that way. But I suppose you are right. I never said I was meek and mild-tempered."

"Me neither. I came up here to get away from all that gushy marriage stuff. It's enough to gag a maggot."

"Oh, and if things had been different, you'd be right there in the midst of all that marriage stuff," he reminded her.

"But they weren't and I'm beginning to believe in divine intervention," she said, finally standing up and getting her crutches positioned just right under her arms.

"What?" Flannon opened the gate for her.

"Looking back, I don't think I had the right kind of feelings for Thomas. I'm still mad at him for not telling me he'd been married; don't get me wrong on that. I'd like to scratch that Southern woman's eyes out and shoot Thomas. But lately I've been . . ." She struggled to find the right words without saying too much. She'd never mention that kiss again, and she sure didn't want him to think she was flirting with him. She'd rather die than let him think that. "Well, I've been noticing what passes between all the newlyweds in Love's Valley. Colum and Ellie. Douglass and Monroe, even after more than a year of being married. Adelida and Rueben. And now Reed and Geneva. I don't think I had that with Thomas. Not that it wouldn't have been a good marriage. It would have. But not an exciting one."

"And you're going to hold out for an exciting one?" Flannon asked, walking slowly beside her down the gently sloping hill.

"I think so," she said, almost giving herself a pat on the back for explaining it so well. But before she could feed her ego too much, her right crutch sunk into a mole hole. She let go of the crutch and grabbed for anything to keep from falling. What she got a firm hold on was Flannon's arm.

In a moment of pure, unadulterated insanity, Flannon threw his arms around Indigo. The momentum of her fall, his off-balance attempt to keep her upright, and the grade of the hill sent them tumbling to the bottom, rolling over and over, tangled up in each other's arms.

Seconds after they stopped rolling, they were surrounded by family and friends, staring down at them as if they were a circus attraction. Indigo was stretched out on top of Flannon. Her full skirt was thrown up over her shoulders and Flannon's face, making a tent of sorts over their upper bodies, her petticoats and pantaloons shining. By the time Reed pushed aside yards and yards of fabric and lace, Flannon was heaving great gulps, trying to refill his lungs with the air that had been knocked from them. Indigo was awkwardly trying to move but having little luck.

"Are you hurt?" Flannon finally gasped.

"No, I'm not hurt. Help me get up. Don't just lie there." She managed to push up and away from him. Was there no mercy for Indigo Hamilton? She'd be the topic of conversation over everyone's supper table again that evening.

"Are either of you hurt?" Colum helped Indigo up first, helping pull down her torn skirt to cover herself.

"I'm not hurt. Crutch hit a mole hole. I want to go home."

"You could have been killed." Colum wrapped Indigo's arm around his shoulders and helped her to the quilt under the trees. "I think we'd better stop by the doctor's house and have him check both of you."

"I'm fine." Flannon sat upright.

"We'll see," Rueben said. "Let's load this stuff up and go by the doctor's. Could have injured something inside, the way you two were rolling down that hill. Besides, Indigo's pride is probably in shambles," he whispered low enough only Flannon heard it. "We'll go now and everyone will wonder if she's hurt again, instead of laughing at that sight of the two of you rolling down the hill."

"Ah, mercy versus ridicule," Flannon said.

Rueben nodded seriously.

An hour later, they'd both been checked by the doctor, declared fit other than a few minor bruises—nothing that wouldn't disappear in a few days' time. Indigo could throw away the crutches and use a walking cane for a few weeks until her foot was fully healed. She was allowed to come down the stairs in the morning and go back up them at night, but not more than that. Her days in the bunk house were finished.

The entire family had packed themselves into the doctor's small waiting parlor while he'd checked Flannon and Indigo. When they filed out, Douglass; Monroe; and their baby, Ford; along with Geneva, Rueben, and their daughter, Angelina all got into the first buggy. Reed and

Adelida sat in the driver's seat and led the way back to Love's Valley.

"Guess we'd better drive this rig home, honey," Colum told Ellie.

"It's a beautiful day and I'd rather be on the driver's seat than inside the buggy," she declared, stepping close enough to her husband that he could put his hands on her waist and lift her up.

Flannon grimaced. He sure didn't want to spend more than an hour inside the buggy with only Indigo, who'd be worse than a bear with an ingrown toenail and a sore tooth after what she'd been through. Truth be known, he surely did not feel like driving all the way home, and the only other option was to ride inside. He held the door for Indigo and helped her like any good Texan would for a lady. Lady, be hanged, that was Indigo.

Indigo vowed she would ride all three miles to Love's Valley without saying a word. At least when she got home, she could sleep in her own bed tonight. The doctor had declared that she was fit enough to climb stairs. She swallowed hard around the lump forming in her throat. She would not weep now. She'd promised herself a good cry when she got home but not until then. The mortification of literally rolling over and over on top of Flannon was over. If there was ever a time to moan and groan, it would have been when her brother pulled her skirt back down to find them wrapped up like two piglets in a blanket.

She busied herself fanning her torn skirt out over the seat and looking out the window. Fall had come to southern Pennsylvania. She would enjoy the bright colors and not think about the disastrous past few weeks. It didn't work. The lovely trees blurred into nothing more than a streak and her thoughts strayed back to the subject at hand, the one sitting right across from her in the buggy, so close she could have reached out and touched that faint bruise forming on his cheekbone. With his Mexican heritage and that lightly toasted skin, would the bruise be darker than the ones on her fair skin? She squeezed her eyes shut and tried her best to blot out the sight of the dimple in his cheek when he smiled. That didn't work either.

"I suppose you'll be happy to get back into your own room," Flannon finally said to break the tense silence. For great pities' sake, he hadn't wrapped his arms around her body and rolled down the little hill in such a disgraceful way on purpose. Nor had he coerced that mole into digging beneath the ground at just that spot so she'd lose her balance.

"Yes, I will. It will be simpler. The girls won't have to bring my things to me all the time. And you won't have to lose any sleep over protecting me. Will you be moving back into the house?"

"No, thank you! I'll just stay in the bunk house as far away from your temper and sharp tongue as possible."

"Some prayers do get answered."

"You pray? I figured you demanded and God was afraid not to deliver."

"Oh, hush. I've been through enough without another fight with you."

Indigo figured he was glad to be rid of her, more than happy to see her go back to her own room. After all, he'd only offered to serve as her protector because he didn't want his family to have to move to the bunk house with her. What was it he'd said when they took the bandages off her head? He'd been the one who offered to shave her head because she didn't like him anyway. And he'd been the one to bring the news her mother was going to Texas for the winter—again, because she didn't like him anyway. So he'd been her bodyguard—because she didn't like him anyway. She'd certainly work on that issue these next few weeks. By spring she'd be glad to see him leave Love's Valley, because by then she really, really wouldn't like him anyway.

Colum drove the buggy down the long, tree-lined lane, around the house, and back to the bunk house before he stopped. Ellie helped Indigo out and took her inside to help take care of the moving process. In the past weeks, more and more of Indigo's possessions had been brought to the little room in the bunk house.

"Want me to help bring your things back to your old room in the house?" Colum asked Flannon.

"No, I've a mind to stay on in the bunk house. I kind of like it out here."

"Then you'd best move into the foreman's room." Colum nodded. Staying away from Indigo wasn't going to help matters one bit, but Flannon would have to figure that out on his own.

"Why's that?"

"Fall has fallen, brother. That means winter is right around the bend. It'll take a lot of wood to keep the whole bunk house warm. Wouldn't take nearly so much to keep you from freezing in the foreman's quarters."

"Winters are bad here, aren't they?" Flannon shivered just thinking about it. He'd spent the last winter of the war in Tennessee and came nigh to freezing to death even there. Pennsylvania was a lot farther north than that.

"If it's anything like last winter, you'll think your blood has frozen in your veins, little brother," Colum said.

"Why do you stay in this forsaken place? Ellie loves you so much, it wouldn't take much sweet-talking to convince her to move to Texas." Flannon pulled a couple of chairs out on the porch, and he and Colum sat down.

"I don't know. It's cold in the winter, all right. Freeze your breath right there before your eyes. But I'm happy here. Really happy, Flannon. I love Ellie and this valley. I think I know what our father meant when he said he loved Ireland with his whole soul, but his heart was in Texas with our mother and he couldn't live without a heart, not even in his beloved Ireland. It's like that with me and Ellie. She'd go to Texas. I have no doubt. But our hearts are all entwined right here in Love's Valley and this winter, we'll be in our own house with lots of love to keep us warm."

"I guess I understand. But I sure couldn't do it. Texas is engrained in me so deep I could never leave it."

Ellie pushed the door open and handed Colum an armload of clothing. "Honey, take these up to Indigo's room, please, and then come back for more. We've got several things to take out of here. Just put them on the bed up there and when she climbs the steps after supper, I'll help her get it all reorganized."

"Give me some too," Flannon said. "Two men can make short work of it."

"Thank you. Sure you feel up to running up and down the stairs?" Ellie asked.

"There's nothing wrong with me. Tomorrow I'll be on the job. I don't reckon my brother here is going to carry everything for me just because I rolled down a hill. In Texas if it ain't bleedin' or broke, then we work. Sometimes we work even if it is." He grinned.

"Then we'll be glad for the help. Follow me and you can take that little nightstand inside." She motioned him inside.

"Pack mules. That's what husbands are," Colum teased.

"Some of us are pack mules without the benefits of someone to keep them warm with their love," Flannon shot back over his shoulder.

"Do something about it then."

"Something about what?" Indigo asked from halfway across the long bunk house main room.

"Nothing," Flannon snapped. He brushed past Indigo, stopping in the middle of the bedroom. "This table?" he asked Ellie.

"That's the one. Here let me unload the top. I'll just put your brush and comb in the drawer, along with this doily and these other things, Indigo. All right, it's ready for you to tote over to the house," Ellie said.

The tension was so thick, it couldn't have been cut with a sharp butcher knife. Ellie chattered on and on about what to do next; they'd need to take the bedsheets off to wash the next morning; would Indigo feel up to helping do laundry; they'd have to go to the attic and find Grandpa Hamilton's walking cane for her.

Indigo avoided looking at Flannon, though his presence was like a blaze engulfing the whole room. Flannon looked around at the room and hoped she didn't forget so much as a hairpin. He'd get over all the infatuation, but he didn't need a thing to set him back in his determination.

Late that night, Indigo hobbled to the window. This was the very spot where she'd been mentally that fatal Sunday afternoon. She and Geneva had been about to make cakes and pies. Everything went black, and she awoke with a sprained ankle and a gunshot wound to her head. She pulled up a rocking chair and eased down into it. The light in the foreman's quarters shone brightly through the window, and she could see Flannon's silhouette through the thin curtains. He took off his shirt and lowered his suspenders. The motions told her he was washing up, getting ready for bed. Soft, sensitive warmth wrapped around her heart like a shroud. She watched from the darkened room until his light went out and didn't move until the moon was high in the fall sky before she went to bed. It wouldn't matter if she dreamed about someone scalping her tonight. Flannon wouldn't hear her cries anymore. Not ever again. He was too far away. She'd already taken her first step to put him out of her mind, and before too long he'd be out of her world.

Flannon stretched out on the cool, clean sheets and shut his eyes. Before long he would have to stoke up a fire in the corner. Colum had been right about keeping the whole place warm. If it truly got as cold as Colum said, that little wood stove out there in the main part of the building wouldn't keep the whole place warm.

Of course, you idiot. That's why there is a foreman's quarters. It's because most of the time all the hired hands didn't stay in the bunk house in the winter, just the spring, summer, and fall. The Hamiltons and one foreman took care of the place through the cold months when nothing could be done anyway. It's not like Texas where we can work all year long.

He sighed deeply. His eyes popped open. He inhaled again. There it was. The smell of the water in Indigo's wash basin. He'd smelled it every morning when Ellie or one of the sisters carried it outside to dump it: something like roses and gardenia mixed together. It had to be his imagination. Indigo had removed everything from the room, and the sheets had been changed.

Still he couldn't sleep for the odor. He flung the covers back and got up without lighting the lamp. He'd follow his nose and not depend on light to show him what was bringing Indigo right into his bedroom. The wash basin wasn't the culprit. He remembered Colum carrying Indigo's matching pitcher and basin with trailing ivy painted on the sides back up to her room. The replacement was blue granite, like a foreman would use. There was nothing on the window sill or on the chair beside his bed.

It had to be a figment of his imagination. He wiped his feet on the hooked rug beside the bed and slipped between the sheets and there it was again, this time even stronger than before. He flipped his body over the side of the bed and looked under it. There in the darkness was an object no bigger than his hand. He reached for it, half expecting a mouse to run the minute it found a human hand coming toward it, but nothing jumped and he brought back a bar of soap. Evidently, Ellie had dropped it from the top of the nightstand when she'd been shoving everything into the drawer.

Flannon righted himself in the bed and sniffed the

soap. Visions of Indigo flooded the dark room. He sighed, lay the soap on the chair beside his bed and shut his eyes. Tomorrow he would give it back to her. But tonight it was his. He shut his eyes and had the most amazing dreams about taming a wild coyote with a broken leg he found in a trap.

Chapter Ten

Ellie had filled the big oval bathtub about half full with cold water and three kettles of water heated on the stove. When steam spewed from the spouts, Indigo carried them carefully to the tub and poured the boiling water in. It would be her first tub bath since the shooting and she fully intended that it be warm enough to last a long, long time. She vowed she'd be wrinkled up like a dried apple before she got out of the water.

She pulled the curtains across kitchen window and shut the door to the dining room. Then she lay her cane aside and began removing her clothing. The day dress lay in a heap on the floor. She untied her petticoat and stepped out of it, leaving the white cotton lawn fluffed up on top of the dress like puffy clouds in a blue sky. She kicked off her slippers and rolled down her stockings, carefully placing them on the chair at the end of the tub. She unfastened a dozen tiny buttons down the front of her camisole and folded it, along with her pantaloons. Then very carefully she sank into the warm water, until the top of her breasts and her head was above water.

"Heaven," she whispered and shut her eyes in pure ecstasy.

Flannon finished his last job in Colum's new house. Tomorrow morning, a man would arrive to do the rest of the finish work: the turned newel post for the end of the staircase, all the baseboards, and the molding around the ceilings. He was the best in the area and his work absolutely beautiful. Flannon could do that type of carpentry but he didn't enjoy it. He'd far rather do the type of work that brought about something to see at the end of each day.

Come morning, Flannon would be at Rueben and Adelida's house, overseeing and working with that crew. The foundation was finished, and the walls for the lower floor were starting up the next day.

The hired hands were working half a day that Monday morning. Jack Dally's trial started in the afternoon, and the whole family would be there: as witnesses, as victims, to give their testimony if needed. The rest of the townfolk would be in attendance for support and to satisfy their curiosity. Things like murders and Klan members didn't reach Shirleysburg very often.

Dinner wouldn't be served under the shade trees that day. The men would leave for Shirleysburg the minute the half-day was finished. The Hamilton and Sullivan ladies had already informed their menfolk that there would be sandwiches in the kitchen at noon, and they were expecting to eat in the hotel dining room at supper. So there would be no cooking in the Hamilton kitchen that day.

Flannon gathered up his tools and organized them in his carpenter's belt, told his brother he was going to the bunk house to get cleaned up, and slowly walked the quarter of a mile back to the house. Winter was edging fall right out of the picture. Some of the trees were already bare. Nothing more than skinny elbows and knees, ashamed in their nakedness reaching out for spring to return in a hurry to reclothe them. A nippy breeze flowed down the valley from the north, sending shivers up Flannon's backbone. Texas got cold in the winter. Blue northers blasted in, bringing cold rain and sometimes even sleet, but it wasn't this kind of cold. Colum said this was just fall in Pennsylvania and not winter at all. Flannon did not look forward to real winter if Colum was telling the truth.

He hurried inside the chilly bunk house and back to his bedroom where he'd made a fire in the stove the night before. It had long since died, leaving only the faintest embers in its wake, but the bedroom was still toasty warm. He hung his hat on the nail to the inside of the door and was removing his coat when he spied the bar of soap beside his blue granite wash basin.

He should have taken it back to Indigo two weeks ago, back when he first found it hiding under his bed, but the time never seemed right. The first day he was busy avoiding her. The second, he started out the door with it in his hand only to change his mind. He'd keep it another day because it made his room smell nice. By the fourth day, he'd realized how personal soap was. It had touched her body. She'd made it with her own blend of scents, and he couldn't just walk in with it in his hand and give it to her in the midst of the other women. There'd be a big to-do about why he hadn't brought it back right away, and then Ellie would look at him again with those questions in her eyes, the ones he didn't want to answer.

Now would be the perfect time to take it back. All the women were at Ellie's house, helping her decide whether to use burgundy or green curtains in her formal living area. Or was it rose or white lace? They'd all been talking so fast and shifting the babies from one to another that Flannon lost all hope of understanding what difference it made anyway. He hadn't seen Indigo in the middle of them, but she was surely there. She wouldn't have been left behind when such earth-shattering decisions were being made.

He'd slip in the back door, lay the soap beside the pump on the dry sink, and disappear. When it turned up, they'd all think Indigo had left it there the last time she washed up. Flannon berated himself for not thinking of such a simple answer to the problem before. It lay in his hand, smooth, aromatic, smelling just like Indigo. Bringing it to his nose, he sniffed the blend of flowers one more time, grabbed his hat before he talked himself into keeping it forever, and marched resolutely up to the back door of the house.

Indigo leaned her head back on the chair at the end of the tub and dozed, savoring every minute of the long, lazy bath. Halfway between being awake and asleep, she heard the back door open but figured Ellie and the women had come home early. They'd see that she was still bathing and rush right back out. Not a one of them would begrudge her a nice soak after the weeks and weeks her ankle had been sprained.

"I'm sorry, I was just bringing . . ." Flannon's feet were

two chunks of lead, glued to the floor. Hot, scarlet color filled his neck and cheeks, and his eyes refused to shut or even blink.

"Oh sweet Mary, Mother of Christ," Indigo caught herself about to jump up out of the water and grab the bath sheet, then sunk as low as she could, only her knees and head left showing. "Get out! What are you doing here anyway?"

Gravity left Flannon's legs and he spun around so quickly that he almost sprouted wings and flew out the back door. "I'm sorry. I was bringing back your soap. I found it under the bed. I didn't know you were bathing. Forgive me. I'll just lay it here on the floor." He stooped to put it down and caught a glimpse of her in the water, her face every bit as red as his.

"Get out!" she hissed.

"Yes, ma'am." He hurried out the back door and across the yard to his quarters as fast as he could run.

When she was sure he was gone, she cautiously stood up and grabbed the sheet, wrapping herself entirely in it. Her mouth turned upward and twitched in a smile. That turned into a giggle, and before long she was sitting in one of the kitchen chairs laughing like a possessed woman as she stared at a bar of soap on the floor.

Poor old Flannon had been as red as a pickled beet, even more embarrassed than she'd been. So he'd found the soap, had he? She'd be willing to bet he'd found it the first night, because she'd made sure it was wet when she slid it under the bed with her crutch. Wet so it would smell just like her right under the very bed where he'd kissed her. It was a mean trick, but she wanted the room to smell all flowery and challenge his masculinity. She'd even entertained notions of Colum giving him a hard time because the room smelled good.

The laughter died. The giggles faded. The smile disappeared. A frown turned the corners of her mouth down. She'd have to face him later that day, and he'd seen her in the bath. Of course, everything was covered but her bare shoulders and neck, then her knees and face. Surely he wouldn't utter a word about it to the fellows. He'd never told anyone about the kiss, and saints above only knew she wouldn't tell a living soul. Her reputation was already in tattered shreds. This would send it to that place where only old maids and nuns lived.

Holding the towel even tighter and picking up her cane, used more for moral support these days than actual need, she made her way up to her room. There she dressed carefully in a dark blue suit with white lapels on the jacket. It was part of her trousseau, the suit she was to have worn on her trip to Philadelphia. Her reflection in the oval mirror on a stand in the corner of her room left no doubt she was still blushing and that her hair hadn't grown enough to draw back into a chignon by any means. She ran a comb through the curls, letting a few fall down on her forehead across the scar. At least her hair was growing, and she found herself dreading the day she'd have to slick it back into a bun at the nape of her neck again. This was so much more carefree and simple.

"Hey, are you in there?" Douglass knocked on her door.

"Yes, come on in," Indigo said.

"I thought you might be getting dressed. Ellie found this soap on the floor. It's dry. We wondered what it was doing there. It's yours, I'm sure. The rest of us don't use gardenia scent in ours. We found what you'd used for your bath down in the bottom of the water. What happened? You wouldn't ever waste good soap by letting it stay in the water like that." Douglass lay it on Indigo's wash stand. "Here, you've missed a button on the back of your skirt. I'll fix it for you."

Indigo muttered, "Don't know about the soap. Maybe it got tangled up in my bath sheet and I dropped it. I don't remember taking two cakes down but then . . ." She left the sentence hanging in midair as she tried to discourage color filling her cheeks again.

"Probably. Well, I just came to see if you needed help. Colum and Monroe are bringing up the buggies. We've talked them into taking us to the hotel tea room for lunch. Not that we had to beg very much. They weren't looking forward to sandwiches one bit. Of course, if we have lunch at the hotel, then we'll have a make-do supper in the kitchen after the trial. Are you nervous about going?"

"Not at all, I want that horrible man to get what's coming to him. Look at my hair! That alone should send him to the gallows. If they'd let me I'd volunteer to be one to pull the rope. I'll be down in just a minute," Indigo said. When Douglass left she spent the next few minutes holding cold compresses on her face to make the red disappear.

As luck would have it, Flannon and Indigo were thrown together at the lunch. Husbands wanted to sit beside wives, those with children especially, to help. By the time everyone was standing behind a chair, there were two, side by side, waiting for Flannon and Indigo. Like a perfect gentleman, he pulled the chair out for Indigo.

"So you think the house will be ready to move into by

Thanksgiving, Flannon?" Ellie asked from right across the table. "We'd love to host the Thanksgiving dinner at our new house."

"Seems like everyone is getting into this Thanksgiving holiday," Flannon mumbled.

"You mean you don't like it? Of course, you wouldn't. What would a Rebel have to be thankful for? You lost your slaves and got whipped soundly in the war," Indigo spit out before she thought. She didn't want to fight with Flannon. She didn't even want to look at him or talk to him.

"Yes, Ellie, I think you can begin to order furniture and all that folderol for your new house," Flannon answered Ellie's question.

Silence prevailed. Everyone waited to see what Flannon would do with Indigo's blunt question.

He answered without looking at here. "Yes, Indigo, I like Thanksgiving. I think it's a wonderful holiday. People should stop and give thanks for what they have and where they've come from. Our country should especially give thanks that we are united once again. I'm thankful for my new nephew, and I hope he and Angelina both have a peaceful world to grow up in and he never has to go to war. I'm thankful for good weather that's let us nearly finish Ellie's house. And I hope it holds out so we can get Rueben's in the dry before the wet and cold stuff gets here."

"That was quite a speech for the brother of few words." Colum grinned.

"Few words!" Indigo smarted off.

Flannon jerked his head around to glare at her. Her face was barely a foot from his. Sun rays, streaming through the window, picked up the copper highlights in all those lovely dark curls and sent flashes of lighter blue through her sapphire-colored eyes.

"Well, he didn't talk much at home," Colum's grin widened. Those two had done nothing but spar since the first day they'd met, an indication they were fighting against something bigger than the both of them.

"Want to explain that little insult?" Flannon asked through gritted teeth. She was punishing him for walking in on her bath. He had apologized so she didn't need to be so snippy. Besides, all he'd seen was a set of healthy-looking knees sticking up out of the water and a floating face.

"You could talk the ears off a billy goat, Flannon Sullivan, and you know it. Colum isn't the only Irishman with the gift of gab. You should be the lawyer in court this afternoon," Indigo said.

"Oh, not me, darlin'. Should be you prosecuting him. With your sharp tongue, you'd cut him to pieces," he said.

They glared without blinking.

Colum chuckled. Monroe roared. Rueben joined in the laughter. And then Reed caught on to what was so funny and he too began to laugh out loud.

"What is so funny?" Geneva asked, wide-eyed. "They were arguing, not telling amusing stories."

"Nothing." Colum wiped his eyes with the white linen napkin. "Let's order now. I think I'll have the roast beef and potatoes."

"And I want the pork chops," Monroe said, hiding behind the menu.

Indigo and Flannon both picked up their menus and went back to pretending the other one was a mile away.

Flannon sighed. Why did she have to smell so good? She looked like a dream in that blue suit, nipped in at her tiny waist. The brief argument only heightened her color, making her more beautiful. He wondered what it would be like to have the privilege of making up after the argument.

Indigo wanted to slap the waitress, who was flirting with Flannon so blatantly it was absurd. Not that she blamed her one bit. The man was handsome in his Sunday suit, dark hair slicked back, brown eyes shining beneath dark ridges of eyebrows. If he ever gave that silly girl one of his smiles, she'd be asking him to meet her in the alley after work hours.

"You, sir?" The waitress batted her eyelashes.

"Roast beef, please," he said, handing her the menu.

"I'll have a chicken salad sandwich and a bowl of noodle soup," Indigo said, shooting the waitress her best drop-dead-on-a-dime look.

"Yes, ma'am. And I'm hoping that mean man who shot you gets found guilty. A woman shouldn't have to worry about going out in her own yard," the waitress said sweetly.

"Why, thank you. But it would have never happened if . . ."

"Indigo." Reed shot his sister a look that spoke volumes.

"I'll be glad when women can speak their minds," she said tartly.

"I'll be back with your food soon as possible," the waitress said as she disappeared back into the kitchen to fix their plates. The daughter of the man who owned the hotel, she worked long hours in the dining room and kitchen, and someday hoped to snag a husband to get her out of Shirleysburg, Pennsylvania. Flannon Sullivan could be just that man if she played her cards right. She'd heard he was from Texas, and it didn't matter one whit to her that he was a Rebel.

They finished lunch just in time to get to the church where the trial would be held. Actually, Reed was the most important witness, since he'd been the one who helped bring Jack to justice in Lynchburg, Virginia, at the time he tried to murder Geneva and Angelina.

By the time the judge was brought into the church, it was packed with townspeople. The Hamiltons and Sullivans occupied the first pews on either side of a center aisle. Jack Dally and his lawyer from Harrisburg sat at the table in the front of the pulpit where a chair had been placed for the judge. There was no trial, though. The judge arrived and did the talking. No witnesses were called. No jury was selected. The judge read a paper signed by the president of the United States and then turned Jack over to four big men, the first recruits of the new secret service organization. The spokesman for the group assured the judge and the family that Jack Dally would not escape this time. They would deliver him directly to the president, and he could cooperate and be sent to Alcatraz, a high-security military prison off the coast of California, to spend the rest of his life behind bars. Or, he could hang if he didn't want to cooperate. Twice he had attempted murder. Once, at least, according to the written statement the president had in his hands, Jack Dally had been among those who'd hanged a man without a trial and for no apparent reason.

The four men chained Jack's hands and feet together and led him out of the church. Pure evil hung over him like a shroud. He grinned wickedly at Geneva as he passed her and snarled his nose at Indigo. He might not escape, but if he ever did, he'd be back and they'd both be dead. His glare chilled both women to the very marrow of their bones.

Indigo wanted to kick the judge or Jack or even Flannon. Anything to vent some of the anger tormenting her insides. That man had caused her no end of grief. He'd almost killed her and given her nightmares. Now he was being led off to be questioned by the president. It wasn't fair. He should have had to stand trial before the Hamilton family for his misdeeds. Geneva should have been able to see the jury bring in a guilty verdict and even watch them build a gallows in the middle of town.

"What do you think, Reed?" Flannon asked when they reached their buggies parked outside the hotel.

"I think that man had better cough up some names, or President Johnson will make sure he spends the rest of his days in prison. Those men won't let him escape, I promise. They're trained and they're professional."

"And there's plenty of them," Geneva said, reassuring herself as much as the rest of the family. "Do you ladies realize we have the rest of the afternoon which was supposed to be spent at the trial? Let's go shopping at the general store. I could use some new cotton lawn. Angelina is already outgrowing her tiny gowns and needs new ones."

"And I want to look at lace for curtains for the parlor," Ellie said.

"I don't need a thing," Indigo said. She didn't want to face any more townspeople. They'd been fortunate in that they'd been the only ones in the hotel tea room at lunch. Everyone else had been home getting ready for the trial or preparing their own luncheon. To go the general store would be disastrous. Every woman in town would have the same idea that Geneva had. They'd gotten their work caught up and now had an afternoon free to shop and gossip.

"I could spend a while at the hardware store," Colum said.

"Flannon, you got anything you need to stay in town for?" Reed asked.

"Not a thing," he said before he put two and two together.

"Then you could take Indigo on back to the valley in one of the buggies. I think if we crowded up, we could make it back in the remaining coach. That way these ladies who want to stay in town can do so, and Indigo can go on home. Guess she wouldn't want to stay up on that foot longer than she'd have to," Reed said.

"Sure," Flannon said wanting to scream that he did not want to take Indigo home. Thank goodness she'd be inside the coach and he'd be driving. He'd let her off at the front of the house, and then he'd take the buggy to the barn where he'd spend a long time getting it unhitched and the horses cared for. After that, he would simply disappear, maybe to check on the foundation of Rueben's house until he was sure the rest of the family was home.

Indigo grimaced but allowed Reed to help her into the buggy. At least she wouldn't have to talk to Flannon or sit beside him on the trip home, where she planned to go straight to her room and read a book all afternoon.

Chapter Eleven

They were halfway to Love's Valley, near the top of the ridge, when the buggy slipped into an enormous pothole right in the middle of the road. Flannon had been so deep in his thoughts, he hadn't even seen the hole and was flung off the wagon to land firmly on his hind end when the back wheel shattered. He hit the road, dust boiling up around him like sifted flour. Before he could even think, the buggy door flew open and Indigo joined him, petticoats fluttering as she plopped right down in his lap with a loud thud.

"We've got to stop meeting like this," he gasped.

"Believe me, it's not on purpose," she snapped.

God, even if you have a sense of humor, this is not funny. I told you, I do not like this man. Why do you keep making all these things happen?

Flannon looked around Indigo at the wagon wheel, busted into so many pieces they'd never be able to use it again. "Guess we either walk or wait," he sighed heavily. There went all his plans for an afternoon of avoiding Indigo. He'd be stuck with her no matter what they did.

"I can't walk that far, so I guess we wait." She put her hands on his broad shoulders and pushed herself into a standing position. "You hurt?"

"No, just my pride. I slid off the seat real easy but couldn't catch myself on a blessed thing." He stood up and brushed the dust from the seat of his dark suit.

"Me too. One minute I was all deep in thought, thinking about all the things I planned to do when we got home, and then I was sliding. Tried to hold onto the seat, but it didn't work. Slid right out of that lousy, ignorant thing."

Flannon grinned. "Lousy, ignorant?"

"That's what Daddy used to say all the time. If it wasn't going to suit him, then it was lousy and ignorant. If it really gave him a problem, it was a lousy ignorant hussy. I'm not sure what it became past that because when it got to that point, I disappeared real quick," she said.

Flannon chuckled.

Indigo giggled.

They were both amazed.

"We can't fix it," he said.

"I know. Guess we'd better make ourselves comfortable until the rest of the family comes to rescue us. Shall we sit over here in the shade of the wagon?"

Before he could answer, ominous black clouds moved over the sun's face, and lightning streaked across the sky in long, jagged lines. A loud pop not so far away said the lightning had found a victim in a big tree. A cold wind whipped Indigo's skirt to one side and ruffled Flannon's hair.

"It's going to rain," Indigo said. "We'll have to try to stay in the wagon, but I don't know how. The slant . . ."

Raindrops as big as dinner plates hit the dirt with enough force to send dust flying in little circles. "We have to try or we'll be soaked." Flannon shoved her inside the coach and tucked her into the fallen side, in the corner. Rain was coming in earnest by the time he got the door shut and wedged himself into the seat next to Indigo. He pulled the heavy drapes to keep out as much of the cold water as possible, throwing the two of them into semi-darkness right there in the middle of the afternoon.

"I'm sorry about the close quarters. It's just that I don't think I could sit anywhere else without sliding out in the rain. I know you'd rather be sitting this close to the devil as me."

"You know something, Flannon Sullivan? You are absolutely right, and it pains me to admit you'd be right about anything."

"I know that. You don't try to hide it, Indigo. But the feeling is mutual," he said, his warm breath tickling the sensitive area behind her ear.

"Why?" she asked.

"Why what?" he countered.

"Why is it we feel this way? I don't like you because you stand for everything I hate. It was your kind that took my brothers off to war. Your kind that burned Ellie's house, that sent the men back maimed or else in memories only. I blame you for everything that had gone wrong all these years from the time I was thirteen. Why do you hate me so badly?"

"I blamed you for taking Douglass from us. She was the only sister and could be as cantankerous as a grizzly bear with a sore toenail, but she was ours. It was your kind that took several of my cousins, who sent more back crippled. I blamed you for taking Colum too. He's always been my very favorite brother and now he's in this God-forsaken place and I'm in Texas."

"Not right now, you're not." She whipped her head around to look at him in flickering lightning.

"I guess not." He looked away to keep from gazing into her deep blue eyes. "But I'll be going back in the spring and there are two holes in our family because of you all."

"I still don't like Southerners," Indigo said honestly. "But somehow, here I am, jilted at the altar, shaved bald, looking at being an old maid right in the face and just now getting enough hair to really cover my head, and suddenly it doesn't seem like such a big deal that my brothers all married Southern women. I'm not going to admit it to them though and if you ever say I said it, I'll say you're lying. I'm beginning to see that the heart has a mind of its own. They're all so happy."

"I won't tell because they'd never believe me. Your actions speak louder than your words, and you act like there's no one on this earth good enough to stand in your presence," he said. Thunder rolled over their heads, and rain pelted the coach like bullets falling from heaven.

"You mean there might be someone out there that good?" she said. She meant for it to come out jokingly. It didn't.

"Not by your standards," he snapped right back at her.

"Flannon, I don't really give a whit what others think of me long as I know I'm right and can look at myself in the mirror and like who's looking back at me."

"Do you really? I don't see how anyone as mean-natured as you are could love herself," he drawled above another clap of thunder.

"Me? You're just like me. Spoiled. Egotistical."

"Me! I'm not egotistical. I don't even have an ego. I'm the youngest of six sons, and before I even could find my place a daughter was born to steal all my thunder. They wouldn't even let me go to war until the last year when I was old enough to go without their permission," he stammered.

"Well, halle-lousy-lujah for that much," she snapped.

"You're the egotistical one. Ego means self. You're the one who was so selfish you'd rather see your brothers married to cold Northern women and live a life of blah before you'd see them married to Southern girls and have all the excitement of a full life."

"I'm not egotistical. I'm sensible. Don't you realize what time it is? It's the second year after the war ended. Feelings are still as raw as the wounds suffered. The country was torn apart, Flannon. Ripped right through her heart and left bleeding. It's not the time for Yankees and Rebels to fall in love. Six years ago, it would have been all right. Six years from now, there might be enough healing to permit it, but not now."

"Tell that to Monroe, or Colum, or even Adelida. Tell them the timing is wrong. You are crazy if you believe that. You said the heart had a mind of its own and shouldn't listen to society or something like that. Then you say it's the wrong time. Which do you really believe? Besides, it's hard to tell someone it won't work when they're living proof that it is."

"I don't know what I believe." She was flustered. Her heart told her one thing. Her mind, quite the opposite.

Her tone caused him to look down at her, all snuggled deep in the downward corner of the carriage. She sounded as if she were truly confused. Her head was tilted to one side, her eyes, lit up by the lightning, were questioning—not him, but herself. He slanted his head just slightly to catch her expression in better light, and then her left arm wrapped itself around his neck, her right one touched his cheek ever so gently, urging his mouth toward full, slightly parted lips.

The kiss rivaled the one they'd shared the night of the nightmare. A white hot explosion somewhere deep down sent heat vibrating through her.

"I'm sorry," he said, finally breaking away from the locked lips. Not because he wanted to, but because it was Indigo Hamilton, for goodness' sake.

"I'm not. I'm not sorry one bit. I wanted to kiss you again to be sure that last one wasn't just a fluke because I was all wrought up over that bad dream. I wanted to see if it really could make me go soft in the brain for a few minutes."

"And did it?"

"Oh, yes, it did, and now I know Thomas Brewster wasn't the man for me. I know I want one who'll make me feel like that. When I go looking for a husband, I'm looking for one who gives me a jolt of desire every time I kiss him. There has to be a fine man in Huntingdon County who can do that, don't you think?"

"I would wish you on no one, not even a Yankee enemy," he said, careful to keep that whoosh of breath from exploding from his lungs in one long gush. If she'd said she was setting her cap for him, he would have gotten out of the carriage and ran all the way to Love's Valley, packed his bags, and walked the whole way back to Texas in a blizzard. Her kisses were the best he'd ever had, but a lifetime with Indigo Hamilton was not in his future plans. Lord, his lifetime would be shortened by half if he ever hooked up with that Yankee witch. She'd cut pieces off his heart each day and throw them back into his face.

"You kiss very well, but you're terrible company. The rain isn't letting up even though the lightning has stopped so I think I'll take a nap."

"Mind if I join you, ma'am?"

"Not one bit. Just don't snore. You know if you'd change places with me, your shoulder would make a nice pillow. Just don't get any funny notions."

It took quite a bit of careful maneuvering, but finally he was shoved down into the corner of the disabled carriage and she was burrowed into his shoulder, his arm tightly around her. In minutes she was sleeping but Flannon was still wide awake. When she began to snore ever so slightly, it was more like a full grown cat purring. She didn't seem nearly as mean.

He finally dozed an hour later, dreaming of Texas and a lady with copper highlights in her long hair. She was sitting with her back to him on the porch with him in a house he didn't recognize, at the base of a mountain covered with trees. Strange, he thought even in his dream, there were no mountains like that in Texas. Not in his part of the state anyway. Rolling hills, green pastures, lots of trees, but no big tall mountains. She had on a bonnet and was busy snapping green beans.

"Flannon, the twins have ridden those ponies long enough. Go make them come in for their baths," she said in his dream.

That's when the door of the carriage opened and Colum stuck his face inside. The dream ended before Flannon could see who it was beneath that bonnet, and he was furious when he awoke.

"Guess you had a little trouble here?"

"Yes, we did." Indigo opened her eyes widely. "The wheel is in shambles. Are the horses all right? We had no choice but to take refuge in the carriage, and that was even precarious. Can you help me out of here, Colum?"

"Sure, and you can squeeze in the coach with the other ladies, and us menfolk will stay and fix this one." Colum eyed his younger brother, who was having trouble waking up.

"How are you going to fix it?" Flannon finally offered no explanation for the way he and Indigo were all nestled together in the corner of the coach.

"Got a spare in the other carriage. Should have put one in this one too, but all four wheels were new on it," Colum said.

"Wouldn't have mattered how old it was when I hit that hole." Flannon took the offered arm and hauled himself out of the coach. The road was muddy, but at least the rain had subsided. "Want me to drive the women home or stay and help?"

"Oh, you're going to stay and help. Ellie can take that carriage on home. It's not that far. I think you've had quite enough of being with Indigo for one day. For a minute there, I could've sworn you two had buried the hatchet."

Flannon shook his head. "It'd take longer than a couple of hours and a lot more than a thunderstorm to make us bury the hatchet. There's still blood in our eyes. You just caught us napping. Everything looks peaceful when it's asleep."

Indigo squeezed into the carriage with the rest of the women. "Where did you put the menfolk? This is a tight fit."

"Oh, it had stopped raining by the time we left Shirleysburg," Douglass said. "Monroe was back here beside me, Reed sat where you are, and Rueben and Colum took the driver's seat. A bit crowded for sure, but we made it. What happened anyway?"

"Buggy hit a hole and the wheel shattered into pieces."

"It's time to replace these old wooden wheels with steel ones," Douglass said.

"Probably so." Indigo nodded.

"So you waited out the rain inside? Didn't the horses throw a fit?" Geneva asked.

"No, strangely enough, they just tucked their heads down and were quiet. Probably scared out of their skins with all that thunder," Indigo said.

"I can't imagine you and Flannon having to spend that much time that close. It's a wonder the whole area isn't on fire from your tempers," Douglass said.

"He does have a wicked temper." She brushed dust from her skirt and bemoaned the mud on the bottom of the skirt. Her petticoats were probably covered in it too. It'd take hours of washing to make them presentable again.

"He has a temper? What about yours?" Geneva asked.

"Mine? I have a reason to be angry. He doesn't. Other than he got his rear whipped in the war and he's up here in my territory. You'd think a Southerner wouldn't want to be here in these times," she said.

"Indigo, that's enough," Douglass said.

"Why? Why is it always enough when I say what I think?"

"In the South, darlin', little girl children are taught tact from birth. By the time they're teenagers, they can tell someone to go to hell and make them look forward to the trip."

"I'm not from the South. In the North we speak our minds."

"Let's change the subject. Indigo, take a lesson from your sisters and learn to mind your wicked tongue," Douglass said. "Now do you think we'll really ever be able to wear skirts that don't drag the ground? Do you think that day will come at the same time we are allowed to wear short hair and not be plagued with having to put it up everyday?"

"Of course," Adelida whispered around Ford's sleeping head. "And we'll be given the right to vote and run for public office, maybe even for president of the United States."

"But not in our day, right?" Indigo asked forlornly.

"No, not in our day," Douglass told her. "But our granddaughters will see the day. We just have to raise our children to be independent and free-thinking, so when the time comes they'll pick up the reins and run with them."

"What did you two do all afternoon?" Geneva asked.

"We fought and we kissed one time," Indigo said bluntly.

All of the other women's mouths dropped in total surprise.

"You what?" Douglass sputtered.

"I kissed him. He didn't kiss me this time. He did one night in the bunk house. I had this horrible nightmare. I guess I was crying out in my sleep, and he came in to waken me. He kissed me, and it turned my toenails to jelly. Lord Almighty, an explosion went off inside me like fireworks. I wondered if it was just because I was having that nightmare and was all afraid. So in the carriage he was really close, and I just wrapped my arm around his neck and kissed him to see if it was the same," she said honestly.

"And?" Geneva smiled brightly. So the little spitfire sister was about to have to eat her words about Rebels.

"And it was the same. So now I'm going to find a man, a Yankee man, who'll make me feel like that. Is that what you all feel when you kiss your husbands?" Indigo's eyebrows drew down seriously.

"Yes, it is," Adelida said. "The first time Rueben kissed me I thought my knees wouldn't hold me up anymore. It was wonderful."

"Me too," Geneva said honestly.

"I cannot believe you kissed my brother." Douglass' crystal clear blue eyes were wider than Indigo had ever seen them.

"Well, you kissed mine," Indigo shot right back at her.

"Yes, but I married yours," Douglass said. "I fell in love with him and would have kissed him everyday, but it took a long time for him to fall in love with me."

"Well, darlin'," Indigo said in a fake Southern drawl, "I

will not marry *your* brother. I couldn't live with that man twenty-four hours without shooting him or poisoning him. We surely weren't meant to be together like the rest of you were. I just intend to find someone who can make me feel like that all the time. I want what you have. I'm glad I didn't marry Thomas because I wouldn't have had a rush of excitement every time he walked in the door. Don't worry, Douglass, I won't be kissing your brother anymore. I've found out what I needed to know. Now I can go find someone who can make me as happy."

Chapter Twelve

"Ah, Mr. Frederic." Ellie crossed the floor with Indigo right behind her. "I'm sorry I wasn't here when you arrived to welcome you. I hope you haven't had a long wait."

"Oh no, Madame, I have not. I've been here but five minutes, and those I've spent looking at these blank walls. Like enormous canvases, they call to me," he said, motioning all around the room with a flourish of arm movements.

"This is my cousin, Indigo. Indigo, this is Jozif Frederic." Ellie made introductions. She'd first met Jozif Frederic before the war when her mother commissioned him to paint a scene on one of her walls. A lovely Garden of Eden scene with trees and grape vines, all dripping with fruit.

"I am pleased to make your acquaintance, Mademoiselle." Jozif bowed before Indigo and cleverly took her hand in his, kissing her fingertips. When he righted himself, he looked into Ellie's clear blue eyes. She'd grown up to be a beauty to be sure, and he'd love to seduce her but she was newly married and although he had no qualms about married women, the look in her eyes said it would be futile to attempt such a mission. The moment her husband entered the room, her eyes were as bright as stars in a midnight sky. Maybe had he been called to paint the walls in two or three years when the bloom was off the honeymoon, he would have had a better chance. But for now he would have to be content with the other one. Indigo, her name was. Her eyes were the color of fine sapphires, and that short hair was more than a little bit enticing. Reckless abandonment, he thought looking at her again. Plus, she was young so she wouldn't know what had hit her. Indigo, a strange name, but it fit her. Ah yes, she would be his diversion while he painted the walls of this enormous room.

"Did my Ellie tell you what she wants?" Colum slipped an arm around his wife's slim waist.

"I was just about to," Ellie said. "You see that view out those windows? I want you to extend it all around this room. I want to feel like I'm standing in the middle of those mountains, but not in the fall. In the spring or summer. You can even paint in a deer or bunnies, or squirrels to make it more realistic. I can just see the room all lit with candles for an evening party, and the feeling of being outdoors in the middle of a cold winter."

"That is very possible, Madame," Jozif said. "As you know, I have studied the art of Fredric Edwin Church. He is known for his Andean panoramas. He painted in Latin America most recently in the heart of the Andes. Also I have worked with Fortunato Arriola, a Mexican painter from San Francisco. When can I begin?"

"Today?" Ellie said.

"Tomorrow." Jozif nodded. "I am staying at the hotel in Shirleysburg. This should take me about a month to six weeks. I shall arrive every morning quite early and stay until it is too dark to paint any longer."

"That will be wonderful," Colum said. For a moment he'd toyed with the idea of telling the painter he could stay in Love's Valley while he was working on the room, but something in the way the man looked at Ellie and at Indigo put him on guard.

"Then tomorrow it will be," Jozif said. "My dear Indigo, would you be so kind as to walk outside with me and show me the different views of the mountains? I might do a few rough sketches this morning while the light is good. You could keep me company."

Jozif Frederic was a fine-looking man. Somewhere between thirty and forty, Indigo would say, with that sprinkling of gray in the temples of his thick, thick black hair. His brown eyes twinkled when he looked at her. Indigo wasn't totally ignorant of the art of flirting, and Jozif was flirting. Even if he was fifteen years older than she was, older than any of her brothers, he'd do just fine for one kiss.

"I'd be delighted to show you the mountains," Indigo said. "But I've got entirely too many chores to waste away the morning watching you sketch. Come along, and you can walk with me halfway to the main house. That would be a good place for you to view the whole valley. Any which way you turn, you can see mountains. The only thing you'll have to use your imagination for is the season. The leaves are all burgundies and oranges right now, so you'll have to think mint green for spring and deeper green for summer."

"With your fresh beauty before me, I'm sure I can think spring and summer." He picked up her hand and laced it through his arm, keeping his hand firmly on hers as he led her out the front door.

"Whew, what was that all about?" Colum asked.

"Flirting with Indigo is what that was about," Ellie said. "We can't have it, Colum. We just can't. I'll tell him I changed my mind and we'll have the wallpaper hangers do these walls as well as the rest of the house. She's too vulnerable right now since the thing with Thomas. He's smooth and much too old for her. He looked at her like he could have her for breakfast."

"Indigo isn't a whimpering little schoolgirl," Colum said. "She can take care of herself. And you'll have your room looking like it was set down in the middle of the mountains. We'll just keep a watch on things. If it gets too heated, we'll do something about it. Now, if I could have you for breakfast . . ." He let the sentence dangle as he drew Ellie into his arms.

Jozif's touch on the soft flesh of Indigo's arm did less than Thomas' did when he draped her arm through his. Yes, this painter was handsome, even pretty with his delicate features and big ebony eyes. His hands were smooth, not rough like Flannon's. Everything about him should have been exciting, the attention, the way he leaned toward her to catch every single word. Somehow it wasn't, but then she'd only just met him. Maybe if he continued to look at her like she was a chocolate bonbon, she'd change her mind. Perhaps fate had thrown him into her pathway since she'd decided to find a man who'd set her heart afire like Flannon did when he kissed her those two times. Whatever fate had in store, there was no use wasting six weeks of precious time flirting around with someone who wouldn't be acceptable anyway.

"And this, sir, is the halfway point. If you turn every which way, like I said earlier, you can see mountains galore. We're not a big valley but a lovely one. The mountains all look pretty much alike but then I suppose all mountains do, whether they're in Pennsylvania or in Latin America."

"Yes, I suppose, and they are lovely, even in their coats of many colors. But they could not ever be as lovely as you, my dear." He turned her gently until her back was against an ancient oak tree. Then with the grace of a dancer he caged her there by putting his hands on the tree at either side of her shoulders.

"You're flattering me." She smiled. It was nice for an older man to pay such attention to her. But, blessed saints, he was a fast mover. She'd figured she'd have to pretend to stumble into his arms or some such thing to get the kiss that morning. Thomas hadn't tried anything this rash until they'd been seeing each other for months. She raised her head to gaze into liquid brown eyes, coming closer and closer. By the time she remembered to shut her eyes, his lips were on hers.

She was putty in his hands. The next few weeks would be quite enjoyable. Indigo Hamilton was ripe fruit, hanging on the tree, begging to be plucked. Perhaps he would even prolong his work, make it last until Christmas so he could enjoy the seduction.

"Ah, my pretty," he whispered, "we are going to have such a nice time while I am here."

"I don't think so." She flattened her hands on his chest and pushed him backward.

It took every ounce of his balancing powers to keep from falling on his rear end right there in the wild ferns growing wild under the trees. "But, my little sweetmeat, you allowed me to kiss you, and we've but known each other a few minutes. Do I do wrong in assuming that you were attracted to me?"

"I guess you do." Indigo put her hands on her hips. "I wasn't attracted to you. Well, maybe a little bit. You are quite handsome, Mr. Frederic, but you know what I felt when you kissed me? Nothing. Not one thing. No soft explosions in my insides, no fireworks, nothing. I intentionally let you kiss me. I'm not a stupid schoolgirl. I knew you'd try something after you lingered over my hand in the house. And I wanted you to kiss me. I really did. But you aren't the one I intend to spend my life with, so it's useless to kiss you anymore."

"Spend your life with!" Jozif exclaimed. "I would not think of such a thing. You are but a child, and I am not a nesting-type man."

"Then you're wasting your time too. I wouldn't be anyone's passing fancy," Indigo said. "Good day, Mr. Frederic. I guess you were looking for a short-term good time. I was just seeing if you could make me all warm and fuzzy with a kiss. Guess we both got our answers. Good luck with your sketches." She turned abruptly and left him standing there in bewilderment.

She stopped by the clotheslines and took in the things that were dry, sprinkling them down and putting them in a bushel basket for the next day's ironing. The house was as quiet as a tomb, giving her time to think about what she'd just allowed. The painter probably did think she was an innocent child who could be seduced quite easily, but she wouldn't be anyone's doxy. She'd just proven one point she'd been worrying about. All kisses weren't the same. The French painter was pretty good, maybe even better than Thomas, but he didn't hold a light to the jolts that shot through her body when Flannon kissed her.

"Got any cold biscuits?" Flannon asked from the back door.

"Speak of the devil."

"Who?"

"Oh, I was just thinking about you, and you appeared out of nowhere," she said honestly.

"Should I run?"

"No and there's leftover biscuits on the table. Didn't you have breakfast?"

"Yes, but I didn't eat enough. My stomach is growling, and dinner is a couple of hours away. What are we having?"

"Pot roast. Today is wash day so we put beef in the oven early in the morning, slice the rest of Friday's bread, and bring in cakes from the well house that we made at the end of the week. You know what we have on Monday. It's the same every week." She picked up the fruit jar with holes punched in the lid and kept sprinkling clothes.

He filled a biscuit with leftover bacon.

"Before you eat that, come here." She motioned to him.

"What for?"

"Because I want you to kiss me."

"You what?" Flannon almost dropped the biscuit.

"I want you to kiss me. Is that so hard to understand?" She glared at him.

"No, I understand that part. But right here? Why?"

"I need to check something."

"What?"

"Well, to be truthful, there's this wonderful feeling when you kiss me. Kind of like everything is all warm and fuzzy inside my heart. I just kissed the French painter who is going to do the walls in Ellie's ballroom. He didn't make me all warm and fuzzy. I want to see if you still do."

"Good Lord!" Flannon dropped the biscuit on the table. "You can't go around kissing every man in the world, Indigo. Has that bullet wound to your head affected your mind?" The vision of seeing that slimy little painter kiss her sent pure green jealousy shooting through him. That he cared enough to be jealous scared him worse than Indigo asking him to kiss her.

"I don't think so. I don't think there's one thing wrong with my mind. It's my heart I'm a bit worried about. Until I can have that warm and fuzzy feeling with a man, then I don't want to waste my time on him. Are you going to kiss me or not?"

"No, I am not," he declared, picking up his biscuit and heading out the back door. "I'm not your puppet, Indigo Hamilton. I won't be kissing you just so you can compare my kisses with other men, and you don't go around kissing every man who comes on the property to see if they can make you all warm and fuzzy. Pretty soon your reputation will be ruined."

"What reputation? If you'll remember, I'm the one left at the altar because my groom's wife came at just the wrong moment. Who's had her head shaved. Who lived with you in the bunk house. Since you are being mean and refusing, I guess you leave me no choice."

"You're not going to go find that old Frenchman and kiss him again, are you? I swear, I'll tell your brothers if you don't stop this nonsense. They may want to put you in a convent."

She grabbed him by the arm and spun him around to face her, taking the biscuit from his hands and tossing it out the open back door to the hounds in one slick movement, leaving him emptyhanded. She wrapped both her arms around his neck and looked deep into those light brown eyes. Just that much was already setting up a bonfire deep inside her. She sunk her fingers into his hair and pulled his face down to hers.

"I guess if you won't kiss me, then I'll have to kiss you."

The whole world stood perfectly still when their lips met. He hugged her close to his chest and her racing heart matched his, beat for beat. He would have never thought to call it a warm, fuzzy feeling, yet there it was. Like the warm heat from a fireplace after being out in the bitter cold all day long . . . beckoning . . . begging for him to come closer for more and more.

"Yes, it's still there," she said, finally pulling out of the embrace, even though she'd have liked to stay there the whole morning. "I'll have that when I find a man for good, or I'll not have anything."

"Are you saying . . . ?"

"I'm saying that I like your kisses. I don't like you. Don't ever plan to like you. But I just wanted to be sure those first two kisses weren't flukes. After all, they were after a nightmare and during a thunderstorm. Could've been the environment. This one was the same. No nightmares. No raging thunder. Just a fantastic kiss. Now make yourself another biscuit and get on out of here."

"You sure you don't want to use me again, just to be sure?" he asked coldly.

"No, I know. You are definitely not the man for me, so there's no need in pursuing this. You are a rotten Rebel and I wouldn't be caught dead with you walking down Main Street of Shirleysburg in anything other than a business arrangement. Go on back to work."

"Well, darlin', I wouldn't want you on my arm in DeKalb, Texas, either. And from now on when I say no to a kiss, I mean it," he said.

Chapter Thirteen

It didn't rain.

That alone was a miracle. The sun rose brightly over the mountains and promised a lovely fall day for the harvest party. The bunk house had been cleaned, all cots removed, and chairs set around the outside edges, leaving the middle for dancing. The house was abuzz with activities as the women prepared the formal dining room for the refreshment center. Tables were set up outside for both lunch and supper. An entire steer had been butchered and, along with two hogs, was being spit-roasted.

The first of the wagons arrived in the middle of the morning, bringing women bearing bowls of potato salad, beans, and fruit salads, along with every kind of dessert imaginable. By lunch time, the huge table in the dining room was laden with nothing but sweets. Four tables outside were covered with dishes, and the aroma of roasting meat filled the whole valley.

"If I could have your attention . . ." Monroe stepped on

the back porch and rang the dinner bell. Where the buzz of gossip and conversation had been rampant, silence prevailed. "I am glad to see so many of you here today. It's been a good number of years since we've hosted a harvest party. It's time that we put the past behind us and began the business of life again. Maybe before we eat, we could have a moment to remember all those who aren't with us anymore. We'll bow in a quiet moment to give thanks for their memories."

The silence was deafening. "Now I'll offer thanks for this meal and we'll go on with our party. Dear Father in Heaven," he began, and Douglass slipped her hand in his. Tonight she'd tell him that Ford was going to have a new baby brother or sister. That was something they could both render up thanks for.

"Amen. Now if anyone goes home hungry after today, it'll be a crying shame and he should be hanged from the neck until dead," Monroe teased. "They tell me the food on the tables out here is nothing compared to the desserts inside. So with the thought in mind that there will be no formal declaration of supper time, let the feasting begin and last until long after the dancing tonight."

Indigo joined four other Love's Valley women behind the table to help serve the long line of people. Two older women, who'd helped with harvest parties in the prewar days, had been hired to wash dishes all day, along with a couple of young women who carried clean plates and silver out and dirty ones in. If it went like it did in the past, there would be a frantic rush to keep plates clean for a couple of hours, then it would be sporadic the rest of the day as people visited, ate a bit, visited some more, and repeated the cycle.

"It looks wonderful," Indigo said.

"I've never seen so much food in my life. Do you really do this every year?" Geneva asked in awe. She'd been the daughter of a tinker, one of the traveling people. They'd made camp in the winter months, and there were people all around them then, but never did they have a party like this. She could scarcely take it all in, nor could she believe that she was one of the hostesses at the affair.

"We used to have one every year. Momma and Daddy would bring me up from Chambersburg and we'd stay a whole week. Aunt Laura always let me help fold napkins. I thought I was the most important person in the whole world," Ellie laughed.

"Looks like a bayou family reunion, only where's the crawdads and rice?" Adelida chimed right in.

"Crawdads?" Indigo snarled her nose.

"Oh, sugar, you ain't had real food yet. Come spring, you and me will go down to the creek and see if we can catch us up some crawdads, and I'll teach you all about the finer foods." Adelida hadn't lost a bit of her deep Cajun brogue.

"We had harvest parties every year until the war," Douglass said. "I love them. All the people. You think they're going to talk to us?"

"Oh, they'll be nice at least to your face. After all, you are Hamiltons and it's your party," Flannon said right behind them. "Besides, little sister, you three Southern women have captivated them with your sweet voices and kindness. It's so unlike Indigo with her sharp tongue and flat accent. By dusk they'll be calling everyone honey and sugar."

"I do not have a sharp tongue or a flat accent," Indigo whipped around and shook a spoon at him.

"Don't bite my head off or beat me to death with that spoon. I'll leave."

She shot him the meanest look she could conjure up and hoped it dropped him graveyard dead on the spot. What a wonderful idea: sacrificing a Rebel to the gods at the end of the harvest party.

"You have pierced my soul with your hateful look." He darted away before she could slap him with the spoon.

"Was that flirting?" Douglass asked.

"It was not!" Indigo turned back to her task. "Just because he kisses good doesn't mean that was flirting."

"He what?" Lizzy whispered from the other side of the table where she'd been loading her plate with everything that looked good. "Did you say he kisses good? I can't believe you'd be kissing anyone after the Thomas Brewster thing. By the way, he and Maudie are here. Have you seen them? They make the cutest couple, and little T. J. is the spitting image of his father."

"Of course I've seen them. I hope they are very happy." She crossed her fingers behind her back and hoped Flannon was right about honey catching flies. "You misunderstood me. I've only heard that Flannon Sullivan kisses good. Isn't that what they say about all Irishmen? They're full of blarney but they kiss good." She'd have to be a whole lot more careful of what she said. She'd let her guard down behind the table with her three sisters-in-law and her cousin Ellie. "How have you been, Lizzy? We'll simply have to find a corner and catch up on what's happened this fall. I've been so busy, I haven't been into town, so you'll have to tell me everything."

"I'll look forward to it," Lizzy's green eyes glistened.

"And you can tell me all about that Flannon Sullivan. I'd just die for a dance with him tonight."

"He's a Rebel and he's half Irish and half Mexican. Your daddy would beat you to death," Indigo said.

"It would be worth it," Lizzy laughed and went to find a seat at one of the tables.

"Like to have gotten caught there, didn't you? Sounds like you don't want him but you sure don't want anyone else to have him." Ellie poked her in the ribs.

"I don't care who has him. I'm just protecting a friend from a definite disaster. Did you notice hardly anyone has said a word about this short haircut? Think it's time to whack off yours?" Indigo changed the subject.

"I'm not brave enough," Ellie said. "What about you all?"

"Holy saints above, Monroe would shoot me," Douglass exclaimed. "I'd love to, if the truth be known, but we got a way to go before that's acceptable in any other circumstance than yours. If you didn't let it grow back out, I'm afraid the whole area would shun you."

"Well, darn," Indigo hissed under her breath.

"And for that too." Ellie narrowed her eyes.

"Well, darn it anyway," Indigo whispered in a singsong whine so low only Ellie could hear. "I'll be good the whole rest of the day, I promise. Guess the long hair keeps my swearing in check too."

"Then it'd better grow fast," Ellie said.

When most of the people were sitting at the tables, lounging on the porch, or under the shade trees enjoying their food, Indigo filled a plate and joined Lizzy at the end of a table.

"Talk to me about that handsome Flannon," Lizzy said the second Indigo got settled into the chair beside her.

"He's Rebel, for great pities' sake, Lizzy. No self-respecting Northern woman would even look at him. Then he's half Irish and half Mexican to boot. Don't be silly. He's just here for the winter, and he's not the man for any Northern woman," Indigo said.

"Honey, I wouldn't care if he was the son of a gypsy tinker and an ex-slave working as a barmaid. He's the prettiest thing I've seen since the war. Even his brother Colum ain't that pretty, and I almost swooned the first time I saw him and Ellie together. No wonder you been keeping him back here in the Valley and not letting him come to town. Women in Shirleysburg would be purring like kittens just to get to walk down the street with him," Lizzy said.

"They wouldn't!"

"Oh, but they would. He's alive, not crippled. He's pretty and he's charming. You just tell him I'm interested and if he wants a few dances later tonight, I'll be standing in line for the honor."

"I certainly will not. I won't have your daddy gunning for me." A bitter jealous streak jabbed her soul. She filled her mouth with sweet potato casserole and half-listened to Lizzy telling her all the news of the town. She'd never been jealous of Thomas. Not until that final five minutes when Maudie reclaimed her rights. Then she'd been furious. But really down-deep jealous? No, not at all. So not wanting Flannon to dance with Lizzy was something of a mystery. Why should she care who he danced with? After all, he was going back to Texas in the spring, and she'd be looking, starting tonight, for another beau.

"Have you heard a thing I've said? Did that shot in your head make you go all daffy at times, Indigo?" Lizzy shook her arm.

"No. I'm sorry. I was thinking about all the little children and getting them down for naps. Remember when we were kids and we had to take naps, and that year Momma let me take one in the wagon with you?" Indigo promised she'd do five more minutes of prayer time to atone for the lies that kept flowing from her mouth that day. It was all Flannon's fault anyway. If he hadn't agreed to stay in the Valley for the winter, none of this would be happening.

"Of course I remember. I thought you were daft then, girl. I would have far rather gone upstairs to your fancy bedroom and took a nap up there, but oh no, you had to sleep in the wagon with the flies and mosquitoes biting us. I'm going in for dessert. I'll take however many plates I can hold to help out." Lizzy gathered six empty plates and a handful of silver on the way down the table.

"So who's your pretty little friend?" Flannon slid into the chair as soon as Lizzy was inside the house. "Are you going to introduce me?"

"To Lizzy? I don't think so. She hates Rebels with a passion. Matter of fact, the only thing she hates worse than a Rebel is an Irishman. She was engaged last year to a man who had about a fourth Irish blood. When she found out about it, she broke the engagement," Indigo said. So, she'd have to spend the whole night in penance. It would be worth it.

"Hmmm, that's strange. She actually winked at me while ago. A bit forward, even for a Northern woman, but then other than you and Ellie, I don't know much about these women up here. Ellie's right nice, but I wouldn't want to judge the rest of the heifers by you. It wouldn't be right to the heifers."

"Are you calling me a cow?"

"If the shoe fits." He grabbed a piece of ham from her plate.

"Stop it. You can't be eating from my plate. People will thing you're courting me. Go away. Everyone knows I'm staying in the house and Jack Dally is gone, so I don't need a bodyguard anymore."

"That is one rule that's the same on both the Rebel and Yankee side of the border," he chuckled.

"We are not courting," she said. "And another thing, don't you ever compare me to a heifer either. I'm not a cow."

"Moo," he whispered, barely audible to even Indigo, as he vacated the spot and went to help carve another ham.

"Did he mention me?" Lizzy returned, all flushed and excited at just seeing him sitting in her chair. "Did you tell him my name? Is he going to come around and ask me for a dance?"

"No, he just stopped by to ask me a couple of questions about where to . . . to . . ." She struggled with another lie and promised she'd only tell the truth the rest of the day if she could find words to finish the sentence. ". . . to put the ham once it was carved. Did we want it in the kitchen and only bring out a plateful at a time, or did we want it all on the tables?"

Lizzy's face fell. "Well, I'm having that dance, with or without your help, Indigo Hamilton. And I'm going to try for the last one of the night. If I didn't know you better, I'd swear you had something for that man. And I'd also swear you have kissed him. Was it good?"

"How would I know? Hey, have you seen that painter who's working on Ellie's house? Want to walk up there and see the wall he has done?" Indigo changed the subject.

"No, I'm waiting until it's all finished and she invites us to tea. And oh my, oh my, that painter is almost as pretty as Flannon Sullivan. He's a little bit old for us. Bet he's all of thirty-five, but the way he looks at a woman just almost melts me in a puddle."

"Lizzy, have you been seeing that man? He's not to be trusted. He's a Frenchman, and you know how they are with words. He could seduce you in a minute," Indigo hissed behind her napkin.

"No, I haven't been seeing him. He's all tied up with the widow Clary. She's more his age anyway, but he sure can make goosebumps on my neck, when he kisses my hand," Lizzy said.

"When did he do that?"

"A while ago. He and the widow are both here, pretending they aren't together. He asked me if I'd like to go with him to see what he painted at Ellie's house, and I figured out right quick what he had in mind, so I declined and told him Ellie would have a party later for us all. But it was exciting, Indigo. Did he ever kiss your hand?" Lizzy nibbled on a piece of shoo-fly pie.

"Yes, he did. I'm not so sure I liked it. How about you?" Indigo said.

"I love it. I wish all men did it. Makes me feel all gushy inside. Like I'm beautiful and they're wanting to . . ." she blushed scarlet.

"Lizzy!"

"Well, darn it. Oops. Don't be telling that I swore, please don't. But I'm the same age as you. Almost twenty. Before the war, we'd have been old maids. I know what men want, Indigo. And I'm tired of waiting around for a man of my own. I'd kidnap that Flannon if I could figure out a way to do it. Carry him off and force him to spend the night with me, then he'd have to marry me, and I could wake up every morning to his pretty face."

"I can't believe what I'm hearing," Indigo groaned.

"Believe it. And one other thing, if I could figure out a way to do it, I'd cut all my hair off too. I just love that look you've got. To think you don't even have to mess with hair pins. I'm pea green with jealousy. You get a legitimate reason to cut your hair and people actually feel sorry for you for it. You get to see that handsome Flannon everyday. If you wanted to, you could go up there to Ellie's and get your hand kissed everyday too. If that's not spoiled, Indigo Hamilton, nothing is. God must like you better than he does me."

Indigo looked up to see Geneva motioning her toward the kitchen, so she made her excuses, promising to look Lizzy up again before the day's end. She did escape before Lizzy demanded again that she drag Flannon back to the table and introduce them. That, Indigo decided, was entirely up to fate. If Flannon was moonstruck by a woman two inches taller than him, then he could introduce himself. Of course, Lizzy was a beauty, with all that creamy skin and no freckles and strawberry blond hair, not to mention her big green eyes. Flannon could do a lot worse if he wanted a sensible woman from the North. But Indigo wasn't encouraging such a thing. No sir, not when she might be in love with the man.

She stopped dead in her tracks just inside the kitchen door. She wasn't in love with Flannon Sullivan. Not in a million years would she admit such a thing. Not after the fit-throwing she'd done when each of her brothers came home with a Southern bride. Not after the misery she'd dealt Ellie when she and Colum were fighting against the love bug. If she was in love with Flannon, then she'd simply have to fall out of love with him, but she wasn't. Jesus, Mary, and Joseph, if he ever got wind that she'd even entertained such a thing, he'd laugh at her.

"Indigo, we need another table cloth for the dining room table. A couple of little boys ate half a chocolate layer cake with their fingers and wiped them on the lace cloth." Geneva pointed to the mess.

"Happens every year," Indigo said. "There's a whole trunk full up in the attic. I'll go up and bring down an armload. Could be we'll need more than one before the day is done. Those little boys will be crying with a bellyache all during naptime. Their mothers will threaten them with a hickory switch, and those two will be a lot more careful. But there are always others."

"How do you do it?"

"Do what?"

"Take all this in stride. I'd be crazy if it weren't for y'all to keep me stable. I could never put on a party like this." Geneva shook her head.

"We've been doing it for years. Grandpa and Grandmother Hamilton's parents started it way back when. It's messy now, but after the party, we'll get everything cleaned up and put away. Those two women in the kitchen are coming back tomorrow to help. And then the tables will be moved into the bunk house this winter for the lunches we serve the hired help. They'll bring in the extra stove stored out in the barn, and we'll do the cooking out there, mainly soups and beans and heavy, hot meals. During the war we didn't have hired help through the winter months, but since then we've got houses to build. Just enjoy the day and don't worry about tablecloths. I'm on my way up to get more."

"Thank you." Geneva shook her head again. It was exciting to be a part of all the plans and the party, but she felt a lot more comfortable sitting in a room alone with Reed and their daughter, Angelina.

Leaning heavily on the railing and going slowly, Indigo made her way up the flight of stairs and to the bedroom where the attic door was located. Surprised to find it slightly ajar, she traipsed up another set of steps. Her ankle had healed, but it still felt weak when she climbed stairs. There was no other choice; Geneva had no idea which trunk Laura stored all the extra tablecloths inside. Ellie would know where to look, but she was outside with Colum, giving little tours of their home to anyone who wanted to take a brief walk that way.

She raised the lid of the trunk and was bent over, carefully lifting three cloths when she felt a presence behind her. Not a noise, but that strange, eerie feeling capable of sending goose bumps up her arms.

"Need some help?" Flannon asked from the far side of the attic where he sat in an old kitchen chair that had long since lost its back.

"What are you doing up here?"

"Staying out of the way of those women."

Sun rays filtered through the window and across his face. If he was pretty an hour ago, he was downright handsome right then. His dimple deepened. His smile widened. Everything about him took her breath away. Just thinking about the way she felt, the way he looked and all the things Lizzy said riled her again.

"Oh, and you are so irresistible that you have to hide from all the women who are trying to drag you to the altar?"

"Looks that way. Make you jealous?"

"I'd have to care about you to be jealous. I haven't signed any contracts about caring about you. You can do whatever you want. Run from the girls. Kiss them. I could care less."

"Oh, my heart is broken." He held his hand to his chest and dropped his head as if in a pout. It only lasted a moment, though, before he gazed back out the window. "Actually, I love this attic. We don't have one in our Texas house. It's all on one floor, and we've got a storage place in the barn for the kind of things y'all toss in the attic. But this is a wonderful place. I found it when I first came here last year. Your momma put me in a bedroom for the night and the door just killed my curious streak. So I opened it and found out I could see everywhere from here."

"No attics?" She gathered the tablecloths up to her chest. "I can't imagine such a thing. Got basements?"

"We don't. Some folks do, I suppose. Hey, come here and look at this. That painter you kissed has your little friend behind a tree and is kissing her hand. I think that's about the third time today. If I didn't know better, I'd swear he was trying to seduce her. And he's seeing some widow too. Boy, he's a sucker for punishment. An older woman and a younger one, both. He'd better be good at sneaking around, and he'd better have lots of energy," Flannon kept his eyes on the people and didn't look at Indigo. Why did fate keep throwing them together? Didn't God know it would take a big man to tame a mean old coyote? He'd actually been hiding up in the attic watching her, but he'd be boiled in hog fat before he let her know it.

She was stunning that day in a deep blue dress sprigged with white flowers and green leaves, and a wide-brimmed straw hat, tied up with a blue satin ribbon under her chin. That tiny waist begging for his hands to span it, her hips swaying every time she moved, her bosom swelling out against the fabric of the dress—if it wasn't Indigo, he'd swear that he was beginning to like her, and that was the craziest notion that had ever entered his head.

Think you can tame a coyote with honey instead of vinegar? Who's to say you're not the man for the job? It'd be a challenge. You could tame her, and the next fellow would be in your debt forever.

Jealousy filled his soul. Envy only meant he did like her in some fashion.

"Oh my, oh my," she gasped when she realized Jozif was indeed getting entirely too friendly with Lizzy. "I've got to get back down there and stop that nonsense. Lizzy wants to be married so badly she's about to get herself into trouble."

He stood up at the same time she turned and for a brief second, their faces were barely inches from each other. He wanted to kiss her, on his own terms, right there in the dusty attic. She wanted to kiss him, on any terms. But the moment passed, and she took flight down the stairs, mumbling something about Geneva needing to redo the table and Lizzy needing her help.

"Save the last dance for me, Flannon. The doctor said I could dance one, so you save that last one for me." She just did it to save Lizzy from another heartwreck. It would be a mercy dance. Like the time she danced with Wallace Wright. All the other girls had avoided him all evening, and she actually felt sorry for the boy.

"Why?"

"Because I said so."

"What if I don't want to? Maybe I want to dance the last one with Lizzy once you save her from ruin."

"Stay away from Lizzy. She's crazy."

That took care of that, Indigo thought, as she helped Geneva remove all the desserts from the table and put on new tablecloths. If he danced the last dance with her, then Lizzy or no one else would coerce him into walking them to their carriage where they could extract an offer for a ride in the country, or issue an invitation for tea after church on Sunday. Indigo was simply protecting her friend from an irresistible Mexican.

Indigo visited with one group, then went on to the next, all afternoon. She and Ellie, as well as Douglass, Adelida, and Geneva tried to be the best hostesses in the county. The first harvest party after the war should be something that would be remembered for years. Besides, it was a wonderful opportunity for the Southern sisters-in-law to carve out a place for themselves with the women of the area. Indigo heard nice things said about the Hamilton women and bit her tongue so many times, she feared she might have to grow a new one. The whole county . . . darn it . . . the whole state could accept those Rebels, but she wouldn't.

Dusk finally settled on the valley. The women took their valises upstairs to the bedrooms, which had been opened to them. Several at a time took turns changing from their day dresses into their Sunday finery for the dance. Indigo chose a dress of scarlet satin, one she was supposed to have worn to the opera on her honeymoon. But that evening when she buttoned all sixty-two small, white satin-covered buttons up the front, her mind was certainly not on Thomas Brewster.

"What a lovely dress," Maudie Brewster said so close behind Indigo that it made her jump. "I love that color, but I could never wear it."

"Of course not, it would bring out every freckle on your face," Indigo said.

"That's what I figured. You're pretty outspoken," Maudie said.

"Yes, I am. And you're all sickening-sweet. You've got Thomas and you got him with your sticky little accent and cute little size."

"I love him, Indigo. I really do, but I'm not a fragile little thing who won't fight for what she wants or to keep what she has. We can be friends, or we can be enemies. I don't really give a darn."

"Keep that attitude and we might be somewhere in between," Indigo chuckled. "You should always wear frothy blue and white. It makes you appear needy and clingy. Men like that. Underneath, we both know you're just like me, don't we?"

"There's no one like you, lady, and I'm not so sure I'd ever want to be. There's not a man in his right mind who'd ever want someone like you."

"Oh, stop your cat fighting," Lizzy said from the other side of the room, where she was struggling with her pink dress trimmed in ecru lace. "Thomas looks at you like he can't wait to get you home and alone. Indigo could have any man on the place. She's already kissed the painter and Flannon Sullivan."

"Lizzy!" Indigo shouted.

The room went silent.

"Well, you have. Tell us what it's like to kiss two men. Which one is better? Was it the painter? Lord, if he mentions Latin America to me again, I'm going to start packing," Lizzy said.

"Wait a minute. You wait a minute, girl. Did Jozif ask you to run away with him to South America?" Indigo cornered Lizzy.

"Yes, he did, but it was just a little joke between us. He's flirting and I'm flirting, but it's not going any further, Indigo," Lizzy said.

"Oh Lizzy, be careful. That man is so slick, he's dangerous. He looks at all young women inappropriately," Maudie said.

"Maybe, but he sure makes us feel like we're alive again, not waiting for the war to end and our men to come home. Did you ever feel like that, Maudie?" Lizzy slipped her feet into pink leather dancing slippers.

"Many times, but that man is evil, Lizzy. Promise us, me and Indigo both, you'll stay away from him. Don't let yourself be coerced into a compromising situation with him," Maudie begged. "Womenfolk are pretty much the same no matter which side their men fought for, and one mishap can ruin you for life."

"Lizzy, on this one issue, Maudie and I are in agreement. Please tell me you won't flirt with him anymore," Indigo said.

"Oh, okay, I promise. Besides, Billy Frank Smith has asked me to dance the last dance with him. You know what that means. He has to walk me to the carriage, and I bet I can sweet-talk him into an invitation for a Sunday afternoon visit if I flutter my eyelashes just right. He's not as pretty as Indigo's Rebel or as smooth as the Frenchman, but he's taller than me and he's been hanging around all afternoon," Lizzy said.

Indigo let loose a whoosh of air. "Thank goodness. Billy Frank is a good man, and you'd do well to go ahead and set your heart for him."

"That's the way I figure it. But you do know that you didn't deny that Flannon is your Rebel? So tell me, did you really kiss him?" Lizzy pried.

"I'm not answering that silly question."

"That means you did, or you would deny it vehemently," Lizzy giggled. "Ladies, let's go show them men down there who's the prettiest three women in the whole state of Pennsylvania."

"I might decide to like you." Indigo looked right into Maudie's eyes.

"I'd like that. Being Southern up here isn't easy right now. I suppose you'd know that better than anyone with those sisters-in-law of yours. I know you were in love with Thomas, but I'd like it if we could at least be civil."

"Civil might be stretching it. For your information, I've realized you were sent here by divine intervention. I wanted to be married, but I don't think I ever loved Thomas. He fought on the right side and he was here."

"Thank you for telling me that."

"Hey, you two, come on. Let's set this dance floor on fire," Lizzy hollered from the hallway.

Flannon knew the moment Indigo walked through the door. He could feel her presence like a wool blanket falling warmly around his shoulders. She flitted from one group to the other, playing the nice hostess. That must put a strain on her heart. Indigo, nice? Tomorrow she'd be worse than a hungry mountain lion after having to be good a whole day and evening. He watched her pat an old man's shoulder, touch an elderly woman's arm as she leaned close to her ear and whispered something that brought on smiles, motion to one of the hired girls to replenish the crystal punch bowl—all with the same grace he'd seen his own mother supervise a harvest party. He had to give it to Indigo: she could pretend to be a lady right well. She did it all without any sign of covering up that mop of curly, short, short hair. She wore confidence well. Why shouldn't she? She was a Hamilton in a part of the world where that meant something.

He slipped out the door and into the shadows on the porch with several other men who hated dancing. There he remained most of the evening, listening to stories of wild horses and wilder women that had to be ninety percent pure, unadulterated lies. When the singer in the band declared that the next dance would be the last one, he moved into the doorway and let his eyes adjust to the flickering candlelight. Indigo's eyes met his halfway across the room and didn't stop staring until she was right in front of him.

"I do believe this is my dance," she said.

"Yes, ma'am, it is."

"Where have you been?" she asked when the slow waltz, a new dance just coming into vogue, began.

"Oh, here and there, taking care of things."

"But you were supposed to enjoy the evening, dancing with all the pretty women. Have you been outside kissing on Lizzy?"

"That's my business. My older brothers taught me when I was very young not to kiss and tell. At least Lizzy's not using me just for comparison purposes."

"You are a bigger rogue than the painter."

"Does dancing the last dance mean I can walk you to the house afterward and ask if I might take you for a drive on Sunday after church?" He expertly changed the subject.

"Why would you do that?"

"Because it's what's expected, isn't it? For the last dance and all. Wouldn't want all these young women here to think the only single hostess can't get a Sunday afternoon ride at the end of the dancing."

"As long as you promise me right here you won't expect a kiss when the ride is finished. I might enjoy a ride but there'll be no kissing, and don't let this let you think I like you one bit either."

"It's a promise."

"I'm not sure I can believe promises anymore. I believed Thomas' promises to love me forever. That lasted until Maudie walked back into his life. What would make me believe your promises?"

"Because my promises are as solid as the Bible."

"Whew, that's quite a statement."

"It's the truth," he said as the song ended. "Now, I'll walk you to the front porch where as hostess, you have to wave at each buggy and wagon as it leaves, I do believe."

"Strange, isn't it? Lots of things are the same in both worlds, aren't they?"

"I think a famous prophet by the name of Flannon Romano Sullivan first made that statement."

"Prophet, huh! More like infamous Rebel. Thank you for the dance and for making me feel pretty."

"You are that, Indigo Hamilton. You can take my word for it that you are indeed the most beautiful flower in the bouquet tonight. Even if I don't like you, it doesn't change the fact you are beautiful."

Taming with honey works better than vinegar.

"I bet it hurt to admit that to me."

"Yes, it did."

She waved like she was supposed to. Her smile stayed plastered on for more than an hour. Her heart was as light as whipped cream on a strawberry tart. Flannon had said she was the prettiest flower in the bouquet that evening. Even if he was a rotten Rebel, he was a man, and he'd said she was beautiful.

Chapter Fourteen

Neither Flannon nor Indigo could believe their good luck. No one lingered over Sunday dinner wanting to talk. Ellie and Colum left, hand in hand, to look at all the progress on their new home. Douglass and Monroe took Ford home to put him down for a nap. Geneva and Reed did the same with Angelina, disappearing upstairs with their daughter as soon as the dishes were finished. Adelida and Rueben declared they were taking a blanket to the creek and taking advantage of what could very well be the last decent day of the year.

"I think you promised me a ride this afternoon," Indigo said.

"Yes, I did. I'll get the buggy ready," Flannon started out the kitchen door.

"No, I don't want a buggy ride. I want to go into Shirleysburg, and if we go unchaperoned in a buggy then there'll be talk. Saddle up our horses. Jewel hasn't been out for a good bout of exercise in weeks. Neither has that black devil you ride. Two people riding horses doesn't mean they're courting, but a closed buggy sure does."

"Good thinking. Meet you in front of the house in twenty minutes?"

"I'll be sitting on the porch."

In a few minutes he led both horses, stepping high, anxious for an afternoon out of the stalls, to the front yard. Indigo had changed into a rust-colored riding habit with a matching deep brown velvet-lined cloak and dark brown soft leather boots. The same wide-brimmed hat she'd worn to the church picnic had a new ribbon, a bright orange one that reminded Flannon of a sugar maple leaf in the autumn.

"Ready?" he asked.

"Yes. I haven't had a good long ride since before the wedding fiasco." She slipped a foot into the stirrup and gracefully slung her body into the side saddle. Someday she hoped it would be proper for a woman to ride astride like a man.

Sure, that'll happen the day after they give us the right to vote, to wear our hair any way we please, to go to college to be lawyers and doctors.

"Penny for your thoughts," he said as they rode side by side up the long lane.

"You don't want to hear my thoughts. It would open up a whole battleground and today I want to ride, enjoy the day, a bit of pleasant conversation, and not fight."

"Will wonders never cease? I thought you lived and breathed to argue and fight. You snap at the other women every chance you get. We can't be in the same room ten seconds without the spark of an argument beginning. What makes you think we can go all day without one?"

"Because it's what I want, and I'm spoiled rotten and get everything I want, according to you." She sniffed the nippy fall air, pulled the cloak a little tighter around her, and ignored him.

"Well, that much is pure gospel. Why are we going to Shirleysburg? I'd figured when we talked about a Sunday ride that we'd just go to the end of the road in the buggy."

"Because this is Sunday afternoon and there are several people I want to visit, beginning with Lizzy."

"Hey, I didn't know we were going to visit. I'm sure not in the mood to go Sunday afternoon visiting. I hated that when Momma made me go with her. 'Sit up straight and be a good boy,' she'd say. That meant sitting on an uncomfortable settee or chair for hours and hours while she talked to the lady of the house about things that did not interest me one bit."

"Me too. I promise the visits won't be more than fifteen minutes each."

"Promises! Made to be broken like pie crust," he moaned.

"So far that's been the story of my life. You just sit up straight and be a good boy," she laughed—not a schoolgirl giggle, not even one of those titters Douglass was capable of putting out when she was nervous or tickled—a real laugh, one from her heart and soul. It was in that moment that Flannon realized what lay deep in his heart, and in the same moment he vowed he'd never admit it to anyone.

"I'll do my best, Momma, but don't get mad at me if I fidget. And can I have two cookies at each place?" he teased.

Indigo laughed even harder. What a complete joy to

throw back her head and let laughter echo up and down the valley.

They rode in silence for more than a mile over the ridge, past the place where the buggy had lost a wheel and they shared that explosive kiss. Just thinking about the experience made Indigo's cheeks glow bright pink.

When they reached Shirleysburg, she pointed to a white two-story house right in the middle of town. "That's our first stop, and it looks like Lizzy is entertaining today. She'd said she and Billy Frank might take a ride, but it looks like her Momma had different ideas. After that I think maybe we'll just have a cup of tea in the hotel. One visiting today will probably be enough."

"Billy Frank? I thought she was trying to get the French painter to notice her." Flannon remembered watching from the attic window and the need to hold Indigo, to kiss her again, but it hadn't happened, and it wouldn't. Grandmother Montoya told him once the story of a wolf that kept coming to the backyard. The owner of the household gave him scraps to tame him so he wouldn't hurt any of the family. The wolf ate the scraps, but he still snarled. Finally, the man realized he was going about it all wrong. If he stopped feeding the wolf, then it would go away forever. That's what Flannon would do with this attraction he had for Indigo. He would stop feeding it after this day. He would be careful not to be in the same room with her without the rest of the family, and he wouldn't offer any more Sunday rides.

Giving up on taming the wild Yank, are you? Hmmm. I figured you were a big enough man to feed the wolf until you had it eating out of your hand.

"Hello," Indigo greeted the young men gathered on the porch. "Is Lizzy receiving today?"

"Yes, she is," Billy Frank said morosely. "We can't even go for a ride until the middle of the afternoon. Her momma says it's not proper."

"Of course it's not. A lady who is receiving has to be home until her hours are over." Indigo shook her finger under his nose.

"Does this mean I don't have to sit up straight and be good?" Flannon asked.

"It means you have a choice. You can stay out here with all these Yankees and take your chances, or you can go inside and sit up straight and be good and let all the women titter around you."

"I'll stay," he said. A porch full of enemy soldiers wouldn't be as bad as a bunch of giggling women.

"Go easy on him, fellows." She knocked lightly on the door and was ushered inside by a dozen voices all speaking at once.

"Whew, I never thought I'd hear Indigo tell anyone to go easy on you. I figured she'd pay us well to murder you and have you buried before she comes out the door. It's no secret that she hates you. After all, you're the one who shaved her head and makes her so mad she could kill you herself if she could get it away with it. So what's going on? She got her cap set for you or you got yours set for her?" Billy Frank asked.

"No, neither one. We're just riding to get us both out of the valley." Flannon leaned against a porch post. "How about you? You got yours set for Lizzy?"

"Have had for a long time. Took that sorry old Frenchy

to wake me up at the harvest party and realize I'd better do something," Billy Frank said.

"Old is right," Flannon grinned.

"You see the way he bends down and kisses women's hands? Man, I'd feel silly doing something like that," Thomas Brewster said from the other corner of the porch.

"Hi there, Thomas. Didn't see you over there," Flannon felt a little more at ease. He'd gotten to know Thomas quite well in the weeks prior to the wedding. Maybe if talk went to war and battles, at least Thomas wouldn't be one wanting to blacken both his eyes.

"I'm here. I'd rather be home, thrown back in my chair, taking a nap. But oh no, Maudie says when a woman is receiving, it's a slap in the face not to go spend a few minutes at her house. Do you know how many are receiving today, Flannon? Six! Even if they only stay fifteen or twenty minutes at each place, that's the whole afternoon. And when it's Maudie's turn, then there goes that afternoon. Makes a grown man wish for a rousing game of baseball. Seems a shame to me that we can't play ball because it's not proper on Sunday but women can sit with their friends and gossip," Thomas moaned.

"Wait until they join ranks and want to vote and run for office and go to college to be doctors and lawyers." Flannon deliberately opened up the debate on women's rights to keep it off the war.

"That ain't going to happen in my lifetime," Billy Frank said. "There's too many men who know what a mess that could bring on. Why, it wouldn't be long until they'd be thinking they didn't need to stay home and take care of their menfolk and kids."

"Reckon it'll ever come about?" Flannon asked.

"It might, but I hope I'm planted six feet under when it does," Thomas said.

"Amen to that," the sheriff said from the corner of the house. "Flannon, you might tell the family in Love's Valley when you get back home this evening that we got word about Jack Dally. He talked all right when it came down to the wire, told names and dates and signed a confession about everything. Trouble was, he never got to that prison in California where they was going to put him. The Klan managed to get inside government prison and took old Jack out and hanged him right in front of a burning cross."

"Whew," Flannon exhaled loudly. "Those fellers didn't take too kindly to him ratting them out, did they?"

"No, they sure didn't. Bunch of fools, but they saved the government from feeding Jack a bunch of meals. Wrong way to go about it, but got the right results, I'd suppose," the sheriff said.

"Hey, what'd you fellows think about us putting together a ball game for next Saturday if it doesn't rain?" Another man asked, changing the mood and the subject.

"Can't. Got the last of the hay to get in if the sun is shining. One more cutting before the winter and I think I'll have enough to last out the cold months," Billy Frank said. "I just wish it wasn't a sin to play ball on Sunday."

Inside the house, ten young women gathered around Indigo, wanting to know what was going on with Flannon Sullivan. Had he talked to Monroe about courting her? After all, he had danced the last dance with her and then walked her to the porch. If he asked her to marry him, would she go off to Texas?

"All right," she held up a hand. "Fact is, Flannon is

my sister-in-law's brother and is staying in the Valley until spring to help build houses and train horses. He's good at both.

So is Colum, his brother. I swear they can put up a house faster than anyone's ever seen. They supervise the hired hands, and it's amazing what they can get done. Same with horses. He could train a horse to bow down and say prayers. Flannon is a Rebel, and there are those among us who haven't had time to forget what that means. I hated him at first and still don't like him. I'm just now to the place where I can almost tolerate my Southern sisters-in-law."

"T. J., darlin', sit up straight now and be good." Maudie pulled her son back up on the settee beside her.

Indigo bit the inside of her lip to keep from laughing loud enough to shatter the windows. Poor little T. J. It would be years before he was big enough to be left in the company of the men on the front porch. Just a toddler, he looked miserable and shoved his thumb into his mouth and began to suck noisily. Had Flannon sucked his thumb? She wondered.

"Indigo?" Lizzy snapped.

"I'm sorry. I was wool gathering. It's been so long since I've been out on Sunday afternoon, I was just thinking about how nice it is to be here," she said.

"Sure you were. You never have a nice thought in your brain. If you did, we'd all run for the hills because it would be the end of the world," Lizzy said. "I was just telling everyone how Jozif tried to kiss me at the party last Saturday and how I slipped right out of his arms. That's when I knew Billy Frank was the man for me. I'm thinking I might like a spring wedding."

"Oh, has Billy Frank already proposed?" Indigo was

glad to get the conversation going in a vein that didn't have a thing to do with her or Flannon.

"Mercy, no, and if he knew I was talking like this he'd run back to Blacklog Valley and hide out until I was too old and feeble to walk down the aisle. He has no idea. But I'm going to let him chase me until I catch him. A spring wedding, though. Mark my words. Maybe late April when everything is turning green. What do you think, Indigo? Would you be my maid of honor? Or maybe by then you'll be married to Flannon and can be my matron of honor?" Lizzy's eyes glistened.

"By then Flannon will be in Texas and I'll be shouting from the rooftops because he's gone," Indigo said.

"If you don't want to stand up with her and Billy Frank, maybe she'll choose me?" Emily Grouse lay her hand on Lizzy's arm.

"I'll be her maid of honor," Indigo said hurriedly. A wedding that went well would take the sting from the one that didn't.

"Oh my, do look at the time. We must be going. There's five more ladies I must visit this afternoon," Maudie said when the clock chimed.

"It's been wonderful, Lizzy," Indigo said.

Lizzy's mother and her friends, who'd been having their own discussion in another sitting room, joined the women in the foyer as everyone was leaving.

"Girl, you are a disgrace with that hair. You should stay at home until it is grown. It would look better for an expecting mother to come to town than for you to be parading about looking like that. Disgraceful is what it is." Mable Cunningham shook her finger at Indigo.

"Oh, it'll grow out, Miz Mable," she said, mocking Douglass' Texas accent.

"And don't you be talkin' to me in that despicable Southern accent neither. Lord help us all, if your mother were here, she'd tan your hide, and you a grown woman. Mark my words, when she gets home she'll straighten out that boar's nest out there in the valley." Mable gave her bony finger one more shake and was out the door before Indigo could say a word.

"Don't pay any attention to her. She's old and will say anything. I still think you've got eyes for Flannon," Lizzy whispered.

"And you've got on rose-colored glasses. Just because you've snagged Billy Frank doesn't mean I have to be next in line. I've had the long engagement, the beautiful wedding. I've heard the promises. I'm not sure I'd ever want any of it again." Indigo tied the ribbon on her straw hat into a wide bow.

"Indigo, if I do get Billy Frank to marry me, can I wear your dress? I'd have to put a lace flounce on the bottom to make it long enough, but there's no way I could ever have one like that unless . . ."

"Honey, if you won't run off with that slimy Frenchman and you'll marry Billy Frank and stay in this area, you can have that dress. Maybe it will bring you more luck that it did me," she said.

"You are a good friend. I'm truly sorry I haven't been out to the valley to visit more since the . . ." Lizzy said.

"Fiasco is what I call it. It happened and I'm over it," Indigo said. "Flannon and I have a long ride back to the Valley and I'm stopping for a cup of tea at the hotel before we go. Come on out to the Valley and see me. I'm not crazy. The disaster didn't cause me to lose my mind. I did lose my hair, but it will grow back and I hope it does it very slowly. You're right. It's sure a lot less trouble."

"Lord, I wish someone would shoot me so I could lose mine and get away with wearing it like you do." Lizzy patted her on the shoulder and went out to the porch to sit in the swing with Billy Frank until the next wave of visitors arrived.

"I wondered if you were going to stay all day," Flannon held out the reins to her horse to her.

"I thought about it, but I promised myself a little time in the hotel tea room, remember?" She hoisted herself into the saddle.

"Come back. You don't have to wait for a receiving day." Lizzy waved from the porch.

"We're really busy in the valley all through the week. You get a chance, you come on out to see me, though. And thank you for the visit." Indigo mounted her horse.

Twenty minutes later, Indigo and Flannon were seated at a table for two in the hotel dining room. White linen covered the table. Matching napkins rested in their laps. A cup of coffee sat in front of Flannon; one of tea sat in front of Indigo.

"So did you men solve all the world's problems out there on the porch?" she asked.

"Sure, we decided to petition the president of the United States and the Good Lord to see if we could play baseball on Sunday afternoons and it not be a sin. It would involve an amendment to the Constitution and the addition of only one little verse in the good book. Amendment would say: Be it known this day by the undersigned good men that it is now legal and not punishable by death on the front porch of a lady's social Sunday afternoon, that men shall be allowed to play baseball on Sunday afternoons providing they have gone to church in the early part of the day and given their first priority that of worshipping God properly. Good book would just say: And God said men could forsake the chattering of women and play ball on Sunday."

"Whew, I don't think I want to be standing beside you on Judgment Day. I do believe that was almost blasphemy."

"It was pure blasphemy, and I will most certainly remember it when I go to confession. And honey, I don't think you've got a snowball's chance in hell of making it to heaven for a judgment. They're going to send you straight to hell."

"Don't you dare talk to me like that. I've got more of a chance than you."

"You are a saint, aren't you? What did you ladies decide? That you would all form a union and fight for the right to vote?"

"I might not be a saint, but I'm not that wicked. No, we didn't talk abut women's rights. Not at a Sunday social. If you promise not to tell, I'll tell you."

"I get to enter the inner sanctum on nothing more than a Rebel's word? An Irishman's word at that? Or even a Mexican's word? You are going to trust my promise?"

"Promise me you won't even tell the men you work with. Not my brothers or, most important, not Billy Frank. I know you don't usually work with him since he's helping the carpenter at Ellie's house, but you have to promise."

"You'd really trust me?"

"You might be the only man I would trust right now.

Even when it's been painful, you've kept your word. Yes, Flannon, I trust you to keep your promises."

"Well then, darlin', you have got my word that I won't breathe a word of what went on in the sanctuary of Lizzy's house."

"Don't be calling me darlin'. I'm not your sweetheart, Flannon Sullivan. The news is that Lizzy and Billy Frank are going to be married in the spring."

"Holy smoke! They only started liking each other at the harvest party. Billy Frank got all jealous when the Frenchy made overtures toward her and finally got up enough nerve to ask her to dance. How did this happen so fast? When did he propose? After church this morning?"

"Billy Frank doesn't even know yet." Indigo leaned back and let that soak in, watching him carefully as it did.

"You mean?"

"I mean." She nodded.

"She's going to chase him until he catches her," Flannon said.

"That's her exact words. Did you hear her say them?"

"No, I've heard it from other women. You wouldn't ever do that would you? Of course not. When you find the man you want, you're so brazen you'll walk up and tell him."

"You got that right. There ain't going to be no chasing involved," she said.

He shook his head. "I do believe you'd do it, Indigo Hamilton."

"You'd better believe it, because I would," she said honestly.

Chapter Fifteen

Six inches of snow blanketed Love's Valley. A slow, steady mist of a rain had fallen all night. Tree branches drooped under the weight. The snap of limbs breaking sounded like gunfire and woke Indigo before daylight. She tried to crawl under her pillow in her half-sleep, thinking Jack Dally had escaped and was shooting at her again. Finally, she realized what was going on and threw back the covers to a chilly room. She grabbed her robe and took off for the kitchen to stoke the fire in the oven. They'd planned a formal family Thanksgiving dinner at Ellie and Colum's new home. Her job was to bring the ham. Ellie had been cooking for days. Today she'd be making pumpkin, chocolate, and lemon pies. Douglass would bring fresh yeast bread, sweet potatoes, and something called pecan pies. Her mother had brought her a big sack of pecans when she'd arrived for the baby's birth and Douglass had been hoarding them like pure gold. Adelida declared she was making some kind of Cajun food.

Geneva had offered to fill in the gaps as she called it, and would be up and around before long.

Indigo drew her shawl closer around her shoulders when she peeped out around the kitchen window curtain. Yellow light from the bunkhouse window gave the snow a golden glow where its rays poured out. The sun arose like a thin lemon wedge, peeping over the mountain top to the east. Ice, wrapped around every tree branch, hugged even the tiniest of limbs and glistened like diamonds in the morning sun rays.

By the time the sun was a full ball of fire sitting on the top of the mountain, Geneva and Adelida had joined her in the kitchen. Reed and Rueben had donned extra clothing and were on their way to the stables to do the morning chores while the three women prepared breakfast. Indigo sorely missed Ellie. Even though her cousin was scarcely half a mile up the valley, it might as well have been all the way to Shirleysburg. Ellie had been her confidant, her sister, her best friend all through the war. Indigo couldn't begrudge her a bit of happiness, but the emptiness in her own heart that morning was a throbbing ache.

Ellie had declared the dinner would be served at noon An hour before, Indigo went to her room to change from work clothes into something more suiting. The women had decided the dinner would be formal, much to the groans and moans of the menfolk, who'd stood together and said it would only be family so they weren't dressing for dinner. By the time the debate ended, a compromise had been reached. The men would dress for dinner, but they could change in the middle of the afternoon.

Indigo opened the doors to the armoire. Several dresses from her trousseau still had never been worn. She fingered a light blue one trimmed in white lace. It had a blue velvet cape to match, but her eye settled on a cobalt blue with long, leg-o-mutton sleeves, a full sweeping skirt with a six-inch flounce at the hem, and a long cape lined in black fur. Flannon had offered to hook up the sleigh and deliver them all right to the front door, so she could wear the fancy slippers she'd had made to go with the dress instead of her sturdy boots.

She looked forward to riding in the sleigh. Adelida had clapped her hands in delight. That woman had been so excited with the first snow the day after Ellie and Colum moved out that she'd clapped her hands like a little child. She'd played so long outside that Rueben had been afraid she'd have frostbite on her fingers and toes. Indigo couldn't imagine a winter in an area like the Louisiana bayou where there was no snow.

Slipping the dress over her head, she viewed herself in the mirror. What would she do with her hair? The dress needed an upsweep with curls at the top and a few sprigs pulled loose to dangle around her face. That was out of the question. She sure wouldn't have a fancy hairdo with nothing to work with but short, bouncy curls. She ran a brush though them but they sprang back to their original, free position. Frustrated at the boyish look, she finally removed the velvet string from the reticule that had been made to match the dress and used it to tie the bangs back off her forehead. The scar had faded very little but Indigo didn't even see it as she looked at her reflection.

She looked at herself in the mirror. "Not bad. At least with a bow tied off to the side I took like I'm female."

By the time she slipped her feet into the slippers, Reed

was calling her name from the foot of the stairs. Flannon was waiting. The ham and several other dishes covered in cozies were already in the sleigh. She needed to quit primping and hurry. That's what he thought. She'd never be beautiful enough. Not if she primped and preened for hours and hours. With all that black hair and her tiny body in that fitted red satin dress, Adelida would make Indigo a wallflower. Then there was Geneva, who'd already decided on a golden dress that highlighted her blond hair and those crystal-clear blue eyes, not to mention Ellie, who would be wearing green and blending right in with all those beautiful walls Jozif had finally finished. Douglass had shown them the dress she intended to wear to the dinner, the very one she'd worn when she danced with the president, and she said she was wearing the mantilla and fancy comb in her hair.

Flannon would never notice her, not with all that beauty surrounding him. She pulled on her gloves and slung the cape around her shoulders.

I don't care what that man notices. If I wanted him, I'd have him, but I'd have to eat so much humble pie after the way I've behaved with the Southerners in this family I'd die from it. So no, thank you. I'm still going to shout from the housetops and dance a jig when he leaves.

"Well, look at my little sister," Reed said. "Almost as pretty as my wife."

Indigo wanted to plead a headache and go to bed but she couldn't do that to Ellie, who'd planned this holiday for weeks, who'd rushed that arrogant, seductive little painter to finish so they could have dinner in her new house. No, she'd just go and be the ugly duckling.

Strange, a person could put all the folderol and finery in a queen's wardrobe on a plain woman and what they had was just a dolled-up plain woman. Not one thing she could put on or hang on her body made her as lovely as any one of the other women who'd be in that gorgeous room today. Southern women! Why did they all have to be so damned pretty?

"Thank you, brother." Indigo forced a smile.

"He's blind as a bat and crazy as a Louisiana bayou 'gator if he thinks anyone is going to outshine you today," Adelida said in her soft Southern voice.

"I thought you were too prim and proper to lie," Indigo said.

"Oh, honey, don't give me attributes like that," Adelida smiled.

"Adelida? Prim and proper? This woman is a shrew," Rueben said.

"Did you tame her?" Indigo said.

"There ain't no one big enough in this world to tame me," Adelida said. "He just learned to love a bayou shrew is all."

Flannon waited in the open sleigh. Geneva and Reed were the first ones out of the house. Angelina was bundled down in half a dozen blankets, with barely a hole left for air. They took up one bench in the sleigh. Rueben helped Adelida to the other bench, then turned around and lifted Indigo to the space right beside Flannon. She was covered from head to foot in blue. All he could see was her beautiful face peeking out from the hood of her fur-lined cape, but he swore he could feel the heat from her body through the layers of fine fabric, even through his own suit and top coat, when her shoulder touched his. For just a moment he could pretend that they belonged together like the other couples.

What in the heck am I doing? I can't pretend any such thing. Her attitude hasn't changed. She'd tear me into little bits and spit me out all across the countryside. There'd be nothing but little bloody chunks of Flannon when she was finished. I could never admit such a thing to her, and you can forget about taming her. God couldn't even do that.

The only outsider at the dinner today would be Flannon Sullivan, and he felt it severely. Maybe that's why Indigo looked good. Even his brother, Colum, and his sister, Douglass, were family now and belonged to Love's Valley. Flannon belonged in Texas, and his heart ached for it.

He admired Indigo. Not many could endure what she had in the past few months and come out on the other side a stronger person. Most would have thrown up their sanity long before now, but Indigo had faced down every obstacle with a good strong attitude and backbone. He drove the distance in silence, enjoying the ride more than he'd thought possible. He'd dreaded that first snow, but it hadn't been so terrible. They'd gotten Rueben and Adelida's house to the point where they could keep working by the warmth of several fireplaces. The bunk house was full to capacity most nights because the hired help didn't want to travel in bad weather, but that was even nice. Flannon spent the evenings listening to tales of hard winters and laughing with his newfound friends, who seemed to have forgotten he wasn't one of them.

Colum met them at the door. "Happy Thanksgiving, everyone. Come in. Come in. Flannon, what do you think of sleigh driving?"

"Horses do the work. I just hold the reins." He said the

first words he'd spoken since Indigo sat down right next to him. "I'll go back and get Douglass, Monroe, and Ford and then put the sleigh and horses in your barn."

"We'll be waiting. Welcome to Thanksgiving. Let me help with those coats. We'll put them in the study. Wonderful day, isn't it? Sun shining, even if it is cold. At least we have a nice warm house and aren't walking out of Blacklog like me and Ellie did last winter."

Ellie shivered with the memory. "I've never been so cold in my life. Come on out in the kitchen, girls. Everything is ready to put on the table. Ham smells wonderful. Colum, you can carve it and put the pieces on that platter with the roses. Reed, the turkey belongs to you. The white platter should hold it. Dark meat on one end. White on the other end. Oh, Adelida, that smells wonderful. What is it?"

"A little andouille jambalaya in that bowl. A little Cajun corn in that one. Next spring I'm going to see if we can grow okra and black-eyed peas in this valley. With some crawdads out of the creek, I can make a decent gumbo," she told them.

"What is this, Geneva?" Ellie uncovered a covered bowl.

"That's peach cobbler. This one is blackberry. And then there's a warm gingerbread with lemon sauce which needs to be put in the warmer to keep it just right. I'm thinking we won't have to cook for the hired help for the whole weekend with all the leftovers we'll have from this meal."

"Maybe the whole week," Indigo said.

Ellie had made placecards, carefully seating everyone around her big table so there would be fathers to help with children if Ford and Angelina weren't happy on the pallets she'd prepared at just the right distance from a roaring blaze in the fireplace. Husbands and wives together. Indigo, where Ellie could keep her from feeling all alone. Flannon, where his sister could keep him happy.

Nothing could be better.

Colum offered grace, and the meal began. Flannon loved the Cajun food, the ham was cooked to perfection, and the wild turkey Reed had shot two days before was moist and delicious.

Indigo tried the Cajun dishes with the idea she would choke the food down to keep from hurting Adelida's feelings, but found herself enjoying the food. She was amazed that she hadn't even gotten angry when Flannon sat down beside her. What could Ellie have been thinking, though? She could actually smell the soap he'd washed with that morning, could feel the heat from his body through his long-sleeved suit coat as his shoulder brushed against hers when they passed dishes around the table.

Lizzy had confided last Sunday that Billy Frank was coming around faster than she'd planned. She just might need Indigo to be her maid of honor by Valentine's Day. Indigo sighed softly. She'd never be a wife. She'd been a bride once, on that disastrous day that seemed like a hundred years ago. But a wife? That would be denied her. The painter hadn't set her heart on pure fire, and she had no doubt none of the other young men in the area would either. Nothing but Flannon's kisses had that power, and she wasn't strong enough to face all family if she admitted she'd fallen for Flannon.

Dinner lasted an eternity. Conversation covered everything from construction of houses, to which the ladies added their opinions openly; to politics in which the ladies didn't back down an inch; to teething babies, when

Reed and Monroe joined right in with their two cents' worth; to recipes, when the men just grunted their approval.

Following dinner, the men retired to the parlor for more coffee while the women cleaned off the table and washed dishes. The afternoon would be lazy visiting. Food would be available for nibbling. Beds were available upstairs for anyone who needed a nap. Ellie had prepared for everything. She didn't intend for one thing to go wrong with her day.

"Did you mean it about a nap?" Flannon yawned.

"There are six bedrooms up there." Colum looked up at the ceiling. "The first one on the left is mine and Ellie's. Anyone of the others could have your name on the pillow. Just go on up and claim whichever one you want."

He chose the one all the way to the end of the hallway on the right, a lovely room with Ellie's touches everywhere: lace doilies on the nightstands, a multicolored quilt on the bed, a small lap throw draped over the rocking chair pulled up to glowing embers in the fireplace. He pulled his boots off, removed his coat, and opened the valise he'd brought from the parlor. He took out his faded work britches, a worn flannel shirt, and suspenders. It took less than two minutes for him to change.

He stretched out on the quilt, pulled the end over his feet, and laced his hands behind his head. Would Indigo agree to let him court her? It was a dumb notion, and he knew the answer. They'd never live through the teasing of the rest of the family after the way they'd ridiculed each other from the first time they met. Something akin to pure hatred had spewed out and covered them both, and they'd never gotten it off. Just when did all these feelings start anyway? He couldn't put a finger on the exact time. It just seemed to grow. Then there was that kiss when she'd had the nightmare, and since that moment it had been impossible to get her out of his mind.

"Oh, excuse me," she said from the doorway.

He hadn't even heard the door open. "I'm not asleep. Come on in."

"I don't think so, Flannon. I can't come into your bedroom and you on the bed. I was just looking for a room for a nap also. I'll go to the room across the hall."

"Then let's sit in the hallway by the window and talk. I'm not sleepy anymore."

"I don't think so, Flannon. They'll be up and down, getting babies to sleep, taking naps. It would look like we were finding a dark corner."

"Then let's go take a sleigh ride. We can go into town. See if Lizzy and Billy Frank want to join us for a ride."

"That would make us courting, now wouldn't it? I'll just go in here and take a nap and you go on back to yours."

"We do need to have a long talk."

"Tomorrow. We'll talk tomorrow. We can't fight on Ellie's day and spoil it."

"Fight?"

"Sure. That's what we do when we talk. Agreements between us are as scarce as hen's teeth." Her voice didn't seem to be nearly as icy or caustic as it had been.

Don't get your hopes up. You don't own enough honey to tame her. She's just being nice because it's a holiday.

"I suppose so. Have a good nap, Indigo. You were the loveliest one of the whole bunch today. 'Bout took my breath away just looking at you."

"Thank you." She softly shut the bedroom door behind her. It wasn't easy leaving him, looking even more handsome in that plaid shirt and sock feet than he'd been in his Sunday finery.

Chapter Sixteen

Indigo tossed and turned, plumped up her pillow, kicked the covers off, and then pulled them back up to her chin. Ellie's whole day had been perfect for everyone but Indigo. Flannon had set her nerves to dancing when she'd found him in the bedroom. She hadn't been able to sleep even though she'd spent an hour in the bedroom across from him. By the time she'd gotten back down to the dining room, Flannon had already given up on his nap and had joined the family in the parlor. She'd helped herself to a bowl of peach cobbler and carried it to the parlor where everyone was talking at once. She loved it. It was the very thing she'd missed all those years when the Valley had been silent except for Ellie, her mother, and herself.

If she acknowledged the feelings she had for Flannon, she'd have to give it all up again. She'd have to go to Texas. To that God-forsaken place that got very little if any snow, where the summer would fry her brain into soft mush, where she'd be the outsider amongst a whole family of Rebels who'd no doubt despise her as much as she had them. She shuddered at the idea of even Flannon's mother. She'd been a lovely lady when she'd visited Douglass and Monroe. Mrs. Sullivan might have a whole different attitude if she looked up one day and there stood Flannon saying he'd taken Indigo Hamilton for a bride.

Her mind went round and round until the moon was a white ball at the top of the sky. The stars hung in their places, looking down on a white-covered valley with long paths cut through it where the sleigh had taken them to and from Ellie and Colum's house. Finally, she wrapped herself in a quilt and pulled the rocking chair close to the window. No light illuminated the window of the bunk house, not a bit of yellow glow to rest upon the glistening snow.

The whole thing was a picture of her heart: one big, cold lump of sadness. No light to shine on it, nothing to make her smile. She drew her bare feet up and gently rocked back and forth for an hour.

Memories began to waltz across her mind, slowly reminding her that the feelings she had hadn't sprung from the clear sky on Thanksgiving Day. They'd started months ago, each one bringing her to the present. Flannon was the one who'd stood up to her and told her she wasn't going to run off with her tail tucked between her legs when she was left at the altar. He'd been the one who shaved her head and was there when the doctor removed the bandages. Not one time did he flinch or look at the ceiling to keep from seeing her in such a pitiful mess. He'd held her and kissed her like she wasn't bald when she'd had the nightmare. He'd made bets to goad her into leaving the valley and going to church. He'd insisted she act as if she didn't give a damn what people thought when her hat blew off at the church picnic, and then handled the matter of rolling down the hill so gentlemanly, no one could find fault with that either. He'd saved the last dance at the harvest party for her and taken her riding the next day so no one would be able to say she was so ugly she couldn't find a beau. He'd told her she was the most beautiful flower in the bouquet.

Very few of the incidents had been done without an argument, but suddenly it was clear to Indigo that that's the way she had to be handled. With her temper, if he'd approached her all sweet and soft, she'd have refused to listen to him. It was battling wills with him that produced results. He understood her because they were just alike, but it could very well be he'd never see it that way.

She picked up her oldest work boots and tiptoed, still wrapped in the quilt, down to the kitchen. She sat down long enough to put them on her chilly feet with no stockings. No use falling and spraining her foot again, now. She couldn't even fake such an injury and need to stay in the bunk house with Flannon. It would be filled with hired hands the next morning if the snow didn't melt. If the old timers were right and the holly bushes were any indication of just how long the snow would last, then they were in for a long, cold winter. According to them, Mother Nature prepared for her feathered creatures in a hard winter by making more berries. If that were truly the case, they might not see bare ground until March. She had lots of time, but she couldn't stand the feeling in her chest that long. It had to be settled now, no matter what the cost.

She slipped out the back door without making a sound and lifted her flannel gown hem and quilt up out of the snow as best she could. She made her way to the bunk house. A rush of semi-warmth greeted her when she opened the door. Cots waited for the men who wanted to stay. On one end, the eating tables were ready to be filled three times a day.

She sat down on the nearest bunk and removed her wet boots. The wooden floor was cold on her bare feet, but she wasn't going to leave a trail of dirty tracks for the men to wonder about come morning. Drawing the quilt tightly around her, she stood at Flannon's door.

She couldn't do it. It was absolutely the craziest idea she'd ever come up with. He'd laugh at her, and that would be worse than a fight. He'd physically throw her out.

She wouldn't do it. She could go back to the house and forget all about her moment of insanity.

She had to do it. She had no choice. She couldn't bear the pain if she didn't.

She had to open the door. It didn't matter how insane it was, if she didn't she'd never have the nerve to try it again.

Besides, her feet were freezing. She turned the knob and waited, shivering from head to toe with a mixture of cold and fear. His room was toasty, the embers of the fire keeping even the floor warm. She shut the door behind her and let her eyes adjust to the room, lit only by dim moonlight filtering through one window. Flannon slept on his back with his arms thrown up under his head. She sat down on the edge of the bed and loosened the quilt she had wrapped around her enough to free her hands.

"Flannon," she whispered, shaking his shoulder.

"What?" He came up out of deep sleep with a jerk, sitting straight up, his nose not an inch from Indigo's. "Who's hurt? What's happened?"

"Nothing. Everything is fine. Please don't laugh at me."

"Why are you here? Why would I laugh at you?" he asked, wiping sleep from his eyes, trying to decide if he was asleep or awake. "It's the middle of the night, Indigo. You're not even dressed? What's going on? What is that you have on?"

"My nightgown and a quilt. I know what time it is, but I couldn't sleep. I've tried to run from it. I've tried to deny it. I've tried everything to get away from it. But I can't. Flannon, I've fallen in love with you. Will you marry me?"

His eyes popped wide open. "Did you just propose to me? Did you say you'd fallen in love with me?"

"Yes, to both." She touched his face.

"So you meant it when you said you'd propose if you found someone to make you swoon when they kissed you. I knew you couldn't resist my kisses," he said, taking her hand in his and holding it against his cheek, liking the way it felt.

"Can't find anyone who can make my knees go weak. Kissed every man in the bunk house last week just to see."

"Indigo!" He was fully awake.

"Well, not really. Couldn't abide those who dipped snuff."

"Did you kiss any of them?"

"Only the one who sleeps in this room. Didn't need to kiss the rest once I figured out the whole thing. So what's your answer, Rebel?"

"I am awake, ain't I? Or is this a dream?"

She pinched his cheek.

"Ouch, guess that answers that question," he said without letting go of her hand. "I realized I fell in love with you a while back, Indigo. Guess I didn't want to admit it either. We'll never hear the end of it."

"Guess not."

"But we're strong, determined people, aren't we?"

"That we are." She leaned forward and kissed him soundly. Yes, the feeling was there, every bit as strong as the other times.

"We'll fight, you know? Just because we admit our feelings doesn't mean we'll never have another argument."

"Ain't a doubt in the world. Is this how we'll make up?"

"I'm not Thomas Brewster. You won't lead me around by the nose," he said, tilting back her face for another kiss.

"And you won't make me some little mousy woman who walks two feet behind you." She put her forehead against his and looked him in the eye.

"I don't think even the angels in heaven could do that, darlin'."

"Then will you marry me?"

"Only if you'll marry me."

"Then we will marry each other. But please let's don't tell the family until it's done. I'll talk to the priest on Sunday after church and when we go for a sleigh ride, if there's still snow, or a buggy ride if not, that afternoon we'll go back to the church and get married."

"No big dress?"

"I've been a bride, Flannon. I want to be a wife. I want to kiss you any time I want," she told him.

"Texas or Love's Valley?"

"You decide and I'll abide. But that's the last decision I'll leave in your hands without an argument," she giggled.

"We'll discuss it later."

"We're really getting married? The Rebel-hating Yank and the Yank-hating Rebel? Do you think we ought to think about it? Did you really fall in love with me? Even with this short hair and my razor-edged tongue?"

"Yes, I did. And you've got my promise that we'll never run out of kisses or love or arguments," he said, and another one of those earth-shattering kisses sealed the promise. He liked her in nothing but a gown and a quilt, admitting that she loved him. Evidently, the coyote was tamed. He hoped not very much, though. He'd never felt as alive in his life as when they were in the middle of a rousing argument.

Indigo touched her lips. They were still warm. She touched his, amazed at how soft they were. He was still a Rebel. He was still an Irishman. He was still a Mexican. He hadn't changed all that much, but she had years and years to work on him. Besides, she wasn't so sure she'd change a thing about him. No one else could make her blood boil with an argument or heat up her insides with kisses. She sure wouldn't live a humdrum life.

She kissed him one more time.

Yes, the fire was there and she expected it would be until they were both old and gray.

Epilogue

Brendon Sullivan helped Laura from the stagecoach in Shirleysburg. She'd spent a wonderful winter in Texas, but if folks wouldn't have thought she'd gone absolutely daft, she would have fallen down and kissed the Pennsylvania dirt the moment her feet hit the ground. Traveling was exciting, but it was good to be home. Spring never looked better.

"Well, well, I do declare, if it's not Laura Hamilton come home to root out that boar's nest out there in the valley," Mable Cunningham said from two feet away.

"Yes, ma'am, I am home," Laura said. "Mable, I'd like to introduce Brendon Sullivan."

"Another one of them Rebels, I'd guess." Mable lowered her snow-white eyebrows at Laura and frowned. "That's what got you into trouble in the first place, Laura Hamilton. Letting that oldest boy of yours marry a Rebel woman. What were you thinking? Why didn't you try to stop it? Harrison would turn over in his grave if he knew the way things are. Minute you left, your daughter lost all her sense. Course one couldn't blame her entirely, being left at the altar by that Thomas Brewster. Wearin' her hair like that. Enticing all the other young women to do the same. And this last stunt! Lo and behold. I'm just glad you're home and can sort it out. But send this one on back where he belongs. Lord have good mercy, but we don't need another one of that kind settling in Love's Valley," Mable mumbled on as she disappeared around the corner.

Laura stood glued to the sidewalk, speechless. "I'm so sorry, Brendon."

"It appears that she's an old woman who says before she thinks. We have those all over the place in our country. What does seem to be the problem?" Brendon took her arm, leading her down the street toward the sign advertising a livery.

"Who knows? Mable never tells all of anything, but from what she says, there's a mess at home and I'll need to straighten it out," Laura said.

"Then I'd suggest we get you home and begin the straightening process," Brendon laughed in a deep, rich tone.

She gave directions, and Brendon drove the open buggy over the ridge and into the valley. Everything seemed the same from the road when they turned down into the lane. She could see Monroe's house from that point. From the last letter she'd had from Ellie and Colum, their house was finished and they were living in it. Rueben and Adelida's was ahead of schedule and they hoped to have it done by early summer, and the foundation was already in place for Geneva and Reed's place. Everything was even neater than the day she'd ridden out of Love's Valley on her way to Texas for a long visit with the Sullivans. What on earth could Mable have been muttering about? Maybe the dear old soul had finally gone crazy.

"Hello!" she called at the front door and motioned Brendon inside. "Hello!" She lay her bonnet on the foyer table and looked up the stairs.

"Mother!" Indigo yelled and ran down the stairs like a common girl rather than a full-grown woman. "You're days early. We'd planned a party for you. Oh, I'm so glad you are home. There are a million things we have to tell you. We'd have written, but we didn't want you to worry," she rambled as she drew her mother into her arms for a hug.

"Indigo, this is Brendon Sullivan. Brendon, my daughter, Indigo." She made introductions as a shiver went up her backbone. Mable had been right. Indigo said there were things they didn't want to write about to avoid worrying her. Just looking at Indigo left no doubt. The girl was radiant. Her hair was short. She looked happy. Something was definitely wrong.

"I'm very glad to make your acquaintance, Indigo. Your mother has talked so much about you this whole trip." Brendon extended his hand and was met with a firm handshake.

"Me too," Indigo told him. Brendon sure wasn't one thing like she'd expected. He looked nothing like Colum or Flannon with that head full of thick red hair iced just a bit in the temples with silver. She'd thought Patrick was the oldest son, but there was so many of them, even if she was in the room with the whole pack of Sullivan sons, she'd probably never keep their names straight. Evidently, Brendon was the oldest and turning gray.

"Mother, you and Brendon wait right here. I'm going to sound the bell. That'll bring them all running. I'm sure glad it's Sunday afternoon. Flannon's just out in the bunk house making sure it's ready for the crew that's coming tomorrow, so he'll be here pretty quick. The rest will take a few minutes," Indigo said.

"Your hair? That scar? What has happened?" Laura finally found her voice. Indigo was happier than she'd ever seen her, but her hair was all gone and a long scar emerged from her hairline and traveled a couple of inches across her forehead.

"We'll explain it all when they get here." Indigo bounced out of the room.

Laura led Brendon to the parlor, and the two of them sat on the settee. A nervous ball of fright filled her breast. Merciful heavens, she'd thought she was bringing home a bit of shocking news. It was looking like she was the one who'd be shocked before the afternoon was finished.

"What are you doing here?" Flannon asked when he burst in the door to the parlor, finding Laura, Indigo, and Brendon all waiting. "We sure weren't expecting to see you, but it's a wonderful surprise."

" 'Tis a long story, Flannon, which I'll tell you as soon as the rest of the family has arrived." Brendon was clearly amused.

"I wish they'd hurry." Indigo's eyes met Flannon's across the room, beckoning him to sit beside her.

He wasn't in a hurry to face his new mother-in-law, so he busied himself bringing in more chairs from the dining room. Brendon and Laura occupied the settee. Indigo sat in one overstuffed chair. That left three more chairs and two rockers. He brought in four chairs. In fifteen minutes the rest of the family had rushed in; hugs were given two and three times.

"Now, let's have it." Laura held Ford on her lap, not believing how big he'd gotten in just six months.

"Who starts first?" Monroe asked.

"You do." Laura narrowed her eyes at her eldest.

"Well, our news that we didn't write to you about in Texas is that Douglass is having another child. She says a girl this time. But Ford told me that he wants a brother, since they're going to be so close in age. Everything else from our personal end of the valley I think we've written and told you," Monroe said.

Douglass left the chair she'd been sitting in and sat on her husband's lap. "I just can't believe you came." She looked across the room at Brendon. "This is such a wonderful surprise. How long can you stay with us?"

"A while," Brendon said.

"Patrick is the only Sullivan who's ever come and left," Flannon said mischievously, hoping Laura picked up the clue and the news of his marriage to Indigo wouldn't shock her into the vapors.

"We'll see," Brendon said.

"Me next?" Rueben asked.

"Yes, but first, congratulations on the good news, Douglass. And I hope you're right about the girl, one we can fuss up with bows and ruffles like Angelina here." She winked at Douglass. At least one of the five hadn't turned the place into what Mable called a boar's nest.

"Okay, we've got a long way on the house, but you already know that. We only saved one little bit of news to deliver today to all of you. Adelida is going to be right behind Douglass on bringing a baby girl into the family. But

I figure it's a boy because Ford is going to need someone to help stand up to the females," Rueben said.

"Oh my, that is wonderful news. Two new babies in one year." Laura beamed.

"Three," Ellie said from the corner, dropping her shawl away from her protruding middle. "Before these two, though. And I don't care if it's a boy or a girl, one of each or a whole litter. I just want lots of them. One a year for a long time. I can't wait for you to come and see our house, Aunt Laura. We had this painter who did the ballroom, and I've got a day's worth of gossip to tell you about that man. But not today. There are too many other things you've got to hear."

"Whew." Laura wiped her brow in mock seriousness. "The valley should be ringing with the laughter of children before many years."

"Now us," Reed said. "Angelina is getting a brother or sister in the early fall. We didn't tell either until you were home."

"Four in one year," Laura laughed. "I never expected a homecoming as great as this. I'm glad none of you wrote me about it because I needed good news today. Mable met our coach and said there were problems out here that I'd need to straighten out. Something about your hair and all these Rebels."

Indigo smiled and got up and went to sit in Flannon's lap. Laura gasped.

"It's all right, Momma. We're legal. And we have the biggest news. Right after you left, this horrid man came to kill Geneva, only he failed. Shot me instead, but don't look so worried, it wasn't anything serious. That's what this scar on my head is all about. Doc and Flannon shaved my head. I was unconscious, or they'd both be dead. Sprained my ankle too and couldn't walk, so Flannon and I lived out in the bunk house. One night I was all upset with nightmares and Flannon kissed me. I wish you could see your face, Mother. You look like you're facing a hurricane. It wasn't that bad . . . at least for an old Rebel. I worked hard not to like him, but I just fell in love with him, and we were married in December. No one knew a thing about it until it was over. Saints above, this whole bunch has given me nothing but grief for marrying a Rebel as it is. I couldn't have stood an engagement and their torment too. So that's our news. Oh, and I guess we'll bring up the tail end of the baby thing this year. I expect you can add a fifth child to that list. Maybe about harvest party time if my calculations are right," she said.

"I'm speechless. I'm not sure I should ever leave this valley again. Please tell me that you are really all right." Laura touched her daughter's arm.

"I'm fine except for this queasy feeling early in the morning," Indigo said.

Everyone in the room laughed except Flannon. "It's not so funny when she tells me to not shake the bed one bit when I'm trying to get out of it. Does that mean you aren't going to shoot me?" he asked Laura.

"Shoot you? Honey, welcome to the family. Are you staying in Love's Valley?" she asked.

"Yes, he is." Indigo beamed. "We're building a Texas house at the far end of the Valley. Right up against the mountains. One floor because Flannon says if I fall and turn my ankle again he doesn't want to carry me up and down stairs. It's going to have a courtyard in the back and a stone wall. We're facing it with field stone we're gathering right here on the property. And that's why the bunk house has to be ready. We've got a crew coming tomorrow morning who's going to work all summer getting these places done. By fall, we'll all be in our own houses and you can have your house back again."

"That will be nice. But this big old rambling place would hold us all as long as you want to stay." Laura handed Ford to Monroe and took Brendon's hand in hers.

The room went deadly quiet.

"Now our news," Brendon said.

"Mother?" Indigo almost stopped breathing.

"Uncle Brendon?" Douglass cocked her head to one side.

"We were married in Texas a month ago. Brendon has given his Ireland business over into the hands of his nephew, Brendon, the Sullivan son who was named for him. He told me when he saw Love's Valley that this was as close to his Ireland as he'd seen and he would be pleased to stay right here with all of us." She leaned over and kissed her groom on the cheek.

He blushed as red as his hair.

"I'd be realizing it will take you a while," he cleared his throat and said in a thick Irish brogue.

"Not me." Flannon grinned.

"Or me." Colum was on his feet and shaking his uncle's hand so fast he almost knocked over the chair.

"I think Douglass has been struck mute, which is a miracle within itself. I never thought anything could render her speechless," Monroe said. "But I'll welcome you and congratulate you both." He hugged his mother and shook Brendon's hand.

“Mother?” Indigo could scarcely believe her ears. “I can’t believe you’d go and marry an Irishman. But I’m not saying a word. At least he’s not a Rebel.”

Reed and Rueben crossed the room together to welcome the newest member into the family. Everyone talked at once when the initial shock wore off and their hearts went back to a steady rhythm.

Laura handed Ford over to Brendon and reached for Angelina. “I think Mable was wrong. I think everything is just right in Love’s Valley. Way I see it, things couldn’t be one bit better.”